Thomas Adolphus Trollope

Beppo the Conscript

A Novel: Vol. I.

Thomas Adolphus Trollope

Beppo the Conscript
A Novel: Vol. I.

ISBN/EAN: 9783337045241

Printed in Europe, USA, Canada, Australia, Japan

Cover: Foto ©Andreas Hilbeck / pixelio.de

More available books at **www.hansebooks.com**

BEPPO THE CONSCRIPT.

A Novel.

BY

T. ADOLPHUS TROLLOPE,

AUTHOR OF "LA BEATA," ETC.

IN TWO VOLUMES.

VOL. I.

LONDON:

CHAPMAN AND HALL, 193, PICCADILLY.

1864.

CONTENTS.

BOOK I.
AT BELLA LUCE.

CHAPTER VIII.

BOOK II.

AT FANO.

CHAPTER I.

CHAPTER II.

CHAPTER III.

CHAPTER IV.

CHAPTER V.

CHAPTER VI.

CHAPTER VII.

BEPPO, THE CONSCRIPT.

BOOK I.
AT BELLA LUCE.

CHAPTER I.
INTRODUCTORY.

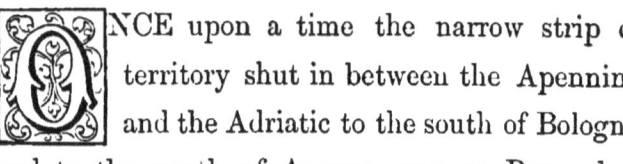NCE upon a time the narrow strip of territory shut in between the Apennine and the Adriatic to the south of Bologna and to the north of Ancona, was, as Byron has written of Venice,

> The pleasant place of all festivity,
> The revel of the earth, the masque of Italy.

That small district, so niggardly squeezed in between the encroaching mountains and the sea, was once one of the high places not only of Italian but of European civilisation. It was there that

the brilliant dynastics of Rovere and Montefeltro
held courts at Pesaro, at Urbino, or a little further
inland among the hills, at Gubbio, which gathered
around them all that was most distinguished in
poesy, in scholarship, in art, and in chivalry. It
was there that Tasso wandered among the green
valleys and by streams made classical for the
second time in their existence, by his genius—
wandered now a brilliant courtier, and now an
outcast mendicant, as the breeze of court favour,
or more surely his own love-sick fancies and
morbid imagination impelled him. There flows
from its ice-cold cradle in the higher Apennine
to its glowing death-bed in the genial Adriatic,
that storied Metauro, whose second golden age,
thanks to the imperishable names and memories
attached to the halcyon days of the Ducal House
of Urbino, has well-nigh eclipsed the glories of
its first. There, mostly on the sea-board of the
Adriatic, are a constellation of cities, once the
chosen abode of the arts, of prosperity, and civilised
culture in every kind ; the rescued fragments of
whose wealth have furnished forth the museums
of every country in Europe, and the story of whose
prime is one with that of the morning-tide vigour
of every liberal art.

It is a different region now! And a very different spectacle, and other ideas and associations, are impressed on the mind of the wanderer among those Adriatic cities! The Church stretched over them its leaden hand, and numbed them! Priestly power came, and literature ceased; education was no more; commerce pined and died; wealth made itself wings and flew away; all energy departed from them; the national character became deteriorated; the cities decayed; palaces fell to ruin; even churches were defaced and their beauty destroyed by the base greed and tasteless vandalism of a clergy, whose scope was to use religion as a begging impostor's swindle. Ever increasing poverty, and the spreading canker of mendicity, invaded fields and cities. Lazy squalor, brutifying superstition, and the degrading and unmanly vices fostered by the morality of the confessional, marked the fallen region as their own!

It was not to be wondered at that a population which had stagnated and languished under priestly government, while the rest of the world had been more or less rapidly and unmistakeably progressing and improving itself, and which had long been hopelessly and fruitlessly beating its maimed and broken wings against the bars of its prison-house, should have seized with boundless enthusiasm the first really promising chance of escape! Nobody was, and only few pretended to be, surprised, when the all but entire population of Romagna rose to welcome their deliverers from the worse than Egyptian bondage under which they had been suffering, and to assist in the not very arduous effort needed for driving their oppressors from the country.

But neither should it have been surprising, though many more persons were surprised at it, that a population, which had grown up under such circumstances, moral and political, should have shown itself, as soon as the first enthusiastic impulse, by which it had achieved its deliverance, was spent, little fitted for the duties and discipline of well-policied political and social life, and above all indisposed for further regularised efforts and sacrifices, the necessity for which was not apparent to them, or at all events did not recommend itself to them as requisite for their own escape from present suffering. There was nothing, I say, in this that might not have been anticipated. As usual, the emancipated slaves thought that every kind of prosperity, happiness, and

well-being was to be the immediate result of their
emancipation ;—that no further self-sacrifice was
needed ; that a millennium of universal cakes and
ale had arrived ;—and all troubles, at all events
all troubles connected with the governing of the
country, had been got rid of for ever.

Of course the disappointment that awaited on
the waking from this dream was great. Of course
a certain measure of discontent with the new
order of things supervened. Of course this was
increased to the utmost, and in every way made
the most of, by those whose interests or prejudices
placed them among the " *laudatores temporis
acti.*" The class which might be so designated in
the Romagna was a very small one. But it was
one that wielded a special and peculiar power ;
for it embraced the very great majority of the
clergy. The clerical government, and its myr-
midons, whether lay or clerical, might be driven
out. But it was impossible to drive out all the
clergy in the country. It was impossible to deprive
parishes of their parish priests. The deposed
government thus left behind it a special and very
effective army, vowed unalterably to its interests.
And this army was composed of a class of men to
whose consciences *all* means were lawful for the

destruction, if possible—for the embarrassment,
if more than that were not possible, of the new
rulers. And it is difficult to exaggerate the power
which such a mass and such a class of irre-
claimable malcontents exercised, when a special
point of attack was offered to them, by any particular subject of discontent felt by the bulk of
the population against any particular part of the
conduct of the new government.

Such a point of attack was offered to them by
the conscription laws.

Military service was in the highest degree repugnant to the feelings of the Romagnole peasant.
He had been used to suffer almost every evil that
could result from bad and oppressive government,
but he had not been used to this. It presented
itself to his mind as a new and unheard-of form of
calamity—a burthen the more intolerable in that
the back had never been trained to bear it. It
was not that the Romagnole peasant is especially
averse from the business of fighting. By no
means so! Call on him to fight for any cause he
approves, there and then, on his own plains and
hillsides, and put his wonted weapon, the knife,
into his hand, and there could be no reason to
complain of his unwillingness to fight. But to

submit to strict discipline, to move at word of command, and above all to go away from family, friends, neighbours, from the well-known and well-loved localities and names into a strange land, this was what was intolerable to the imagination of these people.

But was there any prospect of probability that the Romagnole conscript would be sent forth on foreign service? Was it not for the defence of his native land, for service on Italian ground, that he was needed? Such considerations were urged on the young men of Romagna in vain. Native land! Their native land was Romagna,—the flank of the Apennine, the banks of the Metauro, the shore of the Adriatic, the fat soil and fertile fields which make their district the granary of Italy. To their imagination Piedmont was as much a foreign country as France, or as China! A country the ways and manners, and, above all, the language of which, were utterly and distastefully different from their own.

To be seized and forcibly sent away from his home, from his interests, from his loves, from his habitudes, into an unknown and distant land, where the people were hard and unfriendly by nature (the constant prejudice of Italian provincialism against the inhabitants of other districts), where they talked an unintelligible and disgusting gibberish, where they made bad bread, and grew intolerable wine, and the girls were all ugly, and not kind like the dear ones of their own genial land, this was what the Romagnole youths, especially those of the rural districts, could not make up their minds to endure.

Great, accordingly, was the amount of discontent and trouble occasioned by the inevitable enforcement of the conscription in these districts, and very numerous were the *refrattarj* or runaways, who "took to the hills" rather than submit to the fate which an unlucky number at the drawing of the dreaded conscription had awarded them.

And the natural peculiarities and conformation of their country afforded especial facilities for such means of escape. The fertile low-lands of Romagna are but a narrow strip shut in between the sea and the mountains. The latter are nowhere far off—nowhere beyond the reach of one day's journey on foot. And these mountains represent not only a physical but a political barrier; a frontier which, in the case of the late ill-regulated and ill-agreeing governments of Italy, always involved an extra degree of lawlessness in the habits of the people. The Apennine frontier line between Tuscany and the Papal provinces of the Bolognese and Romagna was always, especially on the Papal side, a district notorious for evil deeds and lawless violence of all kinds. And although the great majority of the Romagnole conscripts, who took to the hills to escape from military service, were for the most part very honest, and in some cases well-to-do country bumpkins, who contemplated no other breach of the law than simple escape from the conscription, yet resistance to the law, and the manner of life to which it necessarily leads, are not good training-schools for the civic virtues. Between breakers of the law, whatever may be the nature of the difference which puts them at odds with it, there is a fellowship and a community of interests which is apt fatally to widen the breach between the law and those whose quarrel with it is of the lesser gravity.

All which, of course, made the disorders arising from the dread of the conscription, prevailing specially among the rustic populations of Romagna, so much the more mischievous and deplorable, and ought to have prevented the ministers of religion, who understood the nature of the case

perfectly in all its bearings, from manifesting their
political hostility to the Italian government by
contributing to place the young men of their
parishes in positions of so much moral danger.

Yet the clergy were everywhere the agents of
and inciters to desertion.

Did a Romish clergy ever yet hesitate to sacrifice morality to a political object ? Their own
reply would be, that they never do so because the
political objects which they have at heart are, in
fact, essential to the good morality of generations
yet unborn, and that whatever sacrifice may be
made of the moral good of present units is justified
and compensated by the advantage gained for
future thousands ;—not to mention that the moral
harm done in the meantime can all be put right
by a stroke of their own art !

Throughout the Romagna, accordingly, during
those first years that followed the incorporation
of that province with the new Italian kingdom,
wherever a conscript wished to abscond instead of
joining the dépôt, his parish priest was ready to
aid and abet his flight ; and wherever his courage
failed to take that step, or his good feeling towards
the new order of things struggled against the
temptation to take it, the priest was at hand

to suggest, to counsel, to persuade, to urge it. Had it not been for the clergy, the evil would have been easily eradicated ; and the state of things in the Romagna, which gave rise to the events related in the following pages, would not have existed.

CHAPTER II.

BELLA LUCE.

HE flat strip of rich alluvial soil at the foot of the hills, and on the sea-shore, which makes the wealth and prosperity of the province of Romagna, is not specially interesting in other than agricultural eyes, save for its numerous and storied cities. The higher Apennine range, which hedges in this district from the rest of the peninsula, is a bleak and barren region for the most part, from which its clothing of forest has, to the great injury of the country in many respects, been stripped in the course of many greedily consuming and improvidently unproducing generations. This rugged backbone of Italy is not devoid in many parts of points of interest and beauty of the wilder and sterner kind; but it cannot be compared, at least in this section of it, with the mountain scenery of either the Alps, the Pyrenees, or even the Jura. But between these two regions there is a third, which teems with beauty and interest of no mean order.

The great massive flanks of the mountains are there broken by an innumerable multitude of small streams into a labyrinth of little valleys,— a world of bosky greenery, of sunny meadows on the uplands, of rich fat pastures in the watered bottoms, of woodlands on the swelling hill-sides. Less valuable as a grain-producing country than the alluvial district along the shore, it is hardly less smiling to the eye of the husbandman; it is far more varied in the nature of its products, and infinitely more beautiful. From many a snug homestead deep-niched in the hollow of some dark-green valley, a peep of the restless Adriatic, tumbling itself into white-crested breakers flashing in the southern sun, is seen across the sea side plains, through the valley's mouth, like the section of a landscape through a telescope. Many a time the storm-wind is sweeping down from the wilderness of the upper Apennine, and teasing the Hadrian sea into meriting its Horatian epithet, "iracundus," while the sheltered nooks among

the lower hills, though they can hear the distant
tempests far above them, and can see the working
of it on the face of the sea far beneath them,
feel nothing of it.

It is not wonderful, that the inhabitants and
tillers of this favoured region should love it, and
be loth to quit it; for it is in truth a lovely
home,—a smiling, grateful, genial, and beautiful
country.

In one of the most beautiful parts of this
beautiful region, a little to the south-west of the
small sea-side town of Fano, and a little to the
north-west of Ancona, there is among the hills a
farm and farmhouse called Bella Luce. "Beautiful
light" is the translation of the name ; and whether
a stranger visited it when the first rays of the
sun, rising out of the Adriatic, were smiling
their morning greeting to it, laughingly peering
round the wood-clothed shoulder of the hill, which
shuts in the entrance to the valley on the southern
side of it ; or whether he saw it at the Ave Maria
hour, when from the cool obscurity of its green
nook it looked ˉout on the last reflected beams
playing with a fitful and fading smile on the
darkening waters, the perfect propriety of the
appellation would hardly be questioned by him.

The little stream, which in the course of ages had hollowed out for itself from the friable side of the Apennine the narrow valley, in which the house and a great part of the farm of Bella Luce are situated, runs into the river Metauro from the north. It falls into the river, that is to say, on its northern side. But as the large valley of the Metauro runs towards the Adriatic not in an easterly, but in a north-easterly direction, and as the small valley opens into the larger one not at right angles, but sloping in a direction from the west, it commanded the peep that has been described of the distant sea.

The farm-house was situated about half-way up the sloping side of the valley, the declivity of which was so shaped that the part above the dwelling was very much less steep than that below it. Immediately in front of the house, which was so placed as to look down the valley, the ground fell away in a descent as steep as it well could be without depriving the soil of its character of pasturage. Had it been steeper, the sod must have been broken by the rains, which are often very violent in this region, and the valley-side would have assumed the character of a precipice. As it was, it was a rich, deeply green,

buttercup-mottled pasture. Above and behind
the house, where the declivity was, as has been
said, very much less rapid, there was a small
quantity of arable land and a wider extent of
wood. Along the sides of the valley below the
farm residence—towards the opening of it, that is
to say—there were several fields mainly of root-
crops ; but the upper part of the valley, beyond
the house, was almost entirely occupied by pasture-
land.

All this constituted a large farm, as the farms
run in that part of the world, and a rich and
valuable one. And Paolo Vanni, the farmer, was
a rich and prosperous man—not so rich and
prosperous as an Englishman might have imagined,
if the long frontage of the farm-house had been
pointed out to him from the opposite side of the
valley, but richer and more prosperous than the
same stranger would have supposed if he had
formed his estimate from a near examination of
the dwelling. In the first case, the imposing
length of the frontage, and the quantity of the
masses of building attached to it, would have led
the Englishman to imagine that none save a man
living in a house with considerable pretensions to
something more than mere comfort, and carrying

on his agricultural operations with a *luxe* of appurtenances and out-buildings of all sorts, could be in the occupation of premises making so great a show. In the second case, he would have marvelled at the quantity of brick and mortar apparently wasted, and would have concluded that only a man whose affairs were going to the bad could be the master of so unrepaired, so untidy, so ramshackle, so poorly-furnished a residence.

Neither conjecture would have hit the truth. Paolo Vanni was of the race of well-to-do peasants —a very common race in the rich and fertile province of Romagna. He was neither better instructed, nor more industrious, nor more enlightened, than any of the peasant farmers of the district, nor differing in his manners and ideas from them. But he held a very good farm—his father and grandfather had held it before him— and he was very fond of saving his money.

The strikingly long front of the building, which makes so magnificent a show from the further side of the valley, resolves itself into elements which have very little of the magnificent about them when seen close at hand. One very large portion of the frontage consisted of an open *loggia*. The *loggia* at Bella Luce occupied one

end of the façade of the building, and consisted of a space enclosed by three solid brick
walls, and in front by a range of five arches
resting on red-brick pilasters. In that one of the
three walls which formed the partition between
the *loggia* and the rest of the house there was a
door of communication, which, by the aid of two
stone steps projecting into the space enclosed, gave
access from the latter to the kitchen of the house.

Most of the *case coloniche*, or farm-houses, in
this part of the country have an open *loggia* of
this sort, half cart-shed, half stable, partly poultry-
house, and partly family sitting-room. And much
pleasanter and wholesomer sitting-rooms such
loggie are in the fine weather, despite the hetero-
geneous uses which they are required to serve,
than the almost always dark, close, and blackened
kitchens. There, in the summer evenings, the
cradle is brought out, and the wife plies her distaff, while the father of the family, and the son,
or the grandfather, or a brother, or a wife's brother
—for these rural families are generally composite,
and consist of more members than a single couple
and their children—are husking a heap of maize,
shot down in a corner, or busy in some other such
task of rural economy. Or, quite as probably,

the male members of the family are smoking their cigars, and enjoying the dear delights of chat and *dolce far niente.*

In contradistinction to the ways of some other districts, the rural habitations of this hill country seem almost always to have been selected with some regard to prospect. Perhaps other more material considerations than the pleasure of the eye may have presided over the selection; but the fact is, that most of these hill farm-houses are so placed that the front commands—as was eminently the case at Bella Luce—a view of more or less extent and beauty. And to a stranger, if possibly not consciously to the inhabitants themselves, a charm is added, which makes some of these picturesquely arched *loggie,*—especially when, as is often the case, a vine is trained around the columns and over the arches,—most agreeable and enticing tempters to an hour of *farniente.*

A large kitchen; a huge room next to it, that served in part as a sleeping-room for a portion of the male inhabitants of the farm, and in part for a store-room for grain; another still larger building used principally as a wood-house, and beyond that a stable for those important members of an Italian *contadino's* family, the oxen, made up the rest of the long façade. But in order to appreciate justly the entire extent of this frontage, it must be borne in mind that each one of all these rooms and buildings was at least twice as large as any Englishman would deem requisite for their respective purposes.

Over the *loggia* there were three good-sized sleeping chambers, two of them, however, accessible only by passing through that nearest to the rest of the house, and the furthest only by passing through both of those which preceded it. It would have been perfectly easy to arrange the two latter in such sort as to have rendered them both accessible from the first. But no such modification had struck the architect, or any of those who had had to use his handiwork, as either necessary or desirable.

Over the huge kitchen was an equally large room, intended apparently, as far as might be judged from the nature of its furniture, as the eating-room of the family. And it was used as such on high days and holidays, and other great occasions, whether the farmer's family had guests on such occasions or not. It was to the solemnity of the occasion, and not to the guests, that the respect manifested by the use of this state chamber was paid. When no such great occasion was to the fore, the great room over the kitchen remained empty of all save its long table and massive benches, and vile French coloured lithographs around the bare yellow washed walls. Above this room was a garret, which served the purpose of a dove-cote. It was the only part of the building that had a second story; and the difference in height thus occasioned broke the outline of the building, as seen from the outside, in a manner very favourable to the picturesqueness of its appearance.

Over the large nondescript room on the other side of the kitchen was a huge chamber, the two windows of which were unglazed, and closable only by heavy, massive, brown-red shutters, opening on the outside. It was unceiled also, and the bare rafters were inhabited and draped by a family of spiders of very ancient lineage. The principal use for which it served was that of a deposit for grain, and at certain periods of the year for various fruits, which were spread out on its wide floor to dry. But there was a bed in one corner, which in very bad weather might appear to some persons a more desirable place of repose than the green hill-side, on which the windows looked.

The other two component parts of the long façade, the wood-house, that is to say, and the stable for the draught-oxen, had no buildings over them ; and the few chambers, which have been mentioned, together with a staircase, which seemed to have been constructed with a view of ascertaining how much space a staircase could be made to occupy, constituted the entirety of the large house, with the exception of certain annexes at the back, which were devoted to divers purposes varying in dignity from that of a back kitchen to that of a pigstye.

It will be understood from the foregoing account, that, notwithstanding the imposing appearance made by Bella Luce when seen from a distance, any tolerably comfortable English farmer lives with a much greater degree of house comfort and convenience than Paolo Vanni. With the one exception of space, every point of comparison would be very much in favour of the Englishman. But ample space is an important element in a dwelling, especially in a southern climate.

But of all the appurtenances and appendages which the English farmer possesses, and the Italian farmer does not possess, that of which the Englishman would least tolerate the absence, and

the presence of which would be least cared for by
the Italian, would be a garden. On that charmingly sheltered hill-side in front of the house, on
that magnificent terrace on either side of it, situations that seem calculated to inspire the idea of
creating a little paradise, if it had never occurred
to any man before, no inhabitant of Bella Luce
has ever dreamed of creating anything of the
kind. Profit has been neglected, as well as pleasure, in this direction. There are no more onions
than roses. Strawberries have been as little
thought of as gilly-flowers! There is an old fig-
tree near one corner of the house; and there is a
grape-vine trained over the pilasters and walls of
the *loggia.* There may be also a patch of potatoes
among other farm crops, and certainly there will
be a crop of some kind of beans, which will contribute to the sustenance of the Bella Luce family.
But that is all. Nothing is more a matter of surprise to an Englishman in Italy, than to find
houses and townlets in the country unable to produce a morsel of fruit or vegetable,—sometimes
not even a potato.

Another large department of rural comforts and
luxuries was almost as much neglected at Bella
Luce as the horticultural. Cheese was the only

form of dairy produce used or cared for by the inmates. They made no butter, and drank no milk, giving to the pigs all that was not converted into cheese.

The Scriptural and classical catalogue, in short, of the oriental cultivator's needs and desires, pretty nearly completed those of Paolo Vanni and his family. Corn, wine, and oil were the main articles on which they subsisted. Meat in no very large proportion, and eggs in somewhat greater abundance, may be added, it is true. And certain moderate supplies of coffee and sugar were brought from neighbouring Fano,—sufficient to give the male heads of the family a little cup of muddy black coffee after their dinner on high days and holidays. The women took none; and the men took it rather as a symbol of feasting and luxury, than because they cared anything about it.

For all that, Paolo Vanni was a warm man,— quite warm enough to have bought up many an English small farmer, who would have most amazingly turned up his nose at the Romagnole farmer's mode of life.

As for the question, however, which of the two, —the English farmer, or the Romagnole agricul-turist,—lived the happier life, and got the greatest amount of satisfaction out of it,—why, that would probably have little to do with the absence or the presence of all that the Englishman could so ill do without; but rather upon matters of a more intimately personal nature ;—with some of which, as regards Paolo Vanni, it is time that the reader should be made acquainted.

CHAPTER III.

AOLO VANNI, to tell the plain truth at once, was not a happy man, very far from it. And the real cause of his discomfort was in fact that "warmness" which has been spoken of. Yet old Paolo was continually laying up treasure where neither moth nor rust doth corrupt. The carefully kept account of the amounts that he had from time to time invested in this way, all duly paid over to heaven's appointed stewards here below, and regularly acknowledged, showed really very considerable investments in that absolutely safe stock. Yet somehow or other the promised satisfaction of mind did not follow from the operation. Perhaps it was that he laid up still larger treasures in the storehouses where moth and rust *do* corrupt, and where thieves *do* break in and steal. But neither the moth nor the rust could much damage old Paolo Vanni's treasure, for it consisted in hard silver dollars; and no thief had ever broken in or stolen from him as yet. It is true, however, that he did strive very pertinaciously to serve two masters. His spiritual guide assured him that this was not only possible, but very easy to be done ; easy at least for him, who had the means to do it. For curiously enough, according to the teaching of Don Evandro Baluffi, the *curato* of Santa Lucia, the more successfully you served Mammon, the more satisfactorily you were enabled thereby to serve God. How was a man to found a perpetual mass, with music and tapers of the larger size—or even without these luxuries, for that matter—if he had not paid sufficient court to Mammon to secure the means of paying for it ? .

Perhaps, however, it is all a matter of proportion. Perhaps Paolo Vanni did not insure highly enough, for he looked on the treasure laid up in purchasing masses and such like, in the light of money paid for insurance ; not exactly against the moth, and the rust, or against thieves, but against certain other contingencies that he had somehow or other learned—assuredly not from Don Evan-

dro!—to fancy might attend the possession of
wealth.

Notwithstanding, however, the kind and constant encouragement of that judicious spiritual
guide, philosopher, and friend, and the undeviating
payment of this insurance money in many forms,
poor old Paolo Vanni, despite his wealth, despite
his thriving and prosperous farm, despite his hale
and vigorous old age, was not contented or happy.
I take it there must have been some importunate
voice, though no one of those about him ever
overheard it, which must have been constantly
earwigging him with doubts and disagreeable
suggestions, of a kind quite opposed to the con-
solatory assurances of the good Don Evandro. But
surely this "voice," whatever it was, could not
have incarnated itself, or rather investmented itself, in a triangular beaver, snuffy black waistcoat,
long-tailed surtout coat, shiny black camlet shorts,
black worsted stockings, and thick, low-cut shoes,
with big plated buckles on them! Surely it did
not come out of any tonsured head on which the
episcopal hand had ever rested in ordination?
Surely it was not the voice of any teacher duly
appointed, authorised, and guaranteed by the
Church; and therefore ought not to have been

listened to for a moment in opposition to Don Evandro, who spoke with all the authcrity that these things could impart? Nevertheless so it was, that old Paolo Vanni, though his sixty odd years sate as lightly on him as sixty years could well sit, though his six feet of height was still a good six feet, undiminished by droop or stoop; and though he could not be said to have been what is usually phrased "unhappy in his family," was a discontented and querulous old man.

There were, however, other causes besides the presence of that importunate voice which I have conjectured might have annoyed him, causes connected with the Bella Luce family politics, which no doubt contributed to this result.

With Assunta Vanni, his old wife, he certainly had no cause to be discontented. Assunta, the sister of a farmer holding a much poorer farm than that of Bella Luce, higher up and further back among the hills, had been a beauty, very tall like her husband, who had also been a remarkably handsome man. This, however, is of less account in a country where beauty, especially of figure and person, is the rule rather than the exception, than it might be considered elsewhere. Sunta had been a good wife, an excellent helpmeet, a

thrifty housewife, and had borne her husband two
children, both boys. What could a wife do more
to merit the admiration of a Romagnole farmer
husband? Moreover Sunta had the highest possible reverence for her lord and master, and
looked on his will as law beyond appeal. If ever
they had any difference of opinion, it was that
whereas Paolo always wished to retain the savings
of the year in the shape of hard cash—*scudi
sonanti,** as the expressive popular Italian phrase
has it,—Sunta would fain have hoarded them in
the shape of additions to her already uselessly
abundant store of house-linen. The difference
had years ago been arranged on the understanding
that all that could be made or saved by the
assiduous labour of the females of the family in
turning flax into yarn, should go to increase the
store in Signora Vanni's presses; always on the
understanding—a point which had given rise to a
slight contest, in which Paolo had been easily
victorious,—that Sunta should herself pay for the
weaving of her yarn in the neighbouring town out
of the proceeds of it.

The labour of the females of the family, I have
said; and have nevertheless mentioned that Sunta

* Sounding crowns.

Vanni was the mother of two sons only. And
doubtless the English reader pictures to himself
Dame Vanni in the similitude of Dame Durden,
who, as the rustic old stave says, "kept five
serving maids." But this would be an error.
Italian farmers, with the exception of a few in a
larger way of business than Paolo Vanni of Bella
Luce, do not in that part of Italy use any labour
on their farms save that of the members of their
family. A large family is held to be a sign and
means of thriving. But it must be a family in
the strict sense of the word, connected by blood,
and not merely by the tie between the employer
and the employed. Whose, then, were the other
fingers besides Dame Vanni's own which assisted
in twirling these ceaseless Bella Luce spindles,
and contributed to the accumulation of sheeting
and table-cloths as little intended to be ever used
as such, as the *rarissimi* of a bibliomaniac's
library to be read? Whose were those active
fingers?

They belonged to Giulia Vanni; and were
among the very few things that Giulia Vanni could
call her own. Giulia was the orphan child of a
distant cousin of Paolo, who was nevertheless his
nearest relative. Paolo was, I think, hardly the

man, at any period of his life, to charge himself
willingly with the support and care of other
people's children. But in the first place it must
be understood that public opinion, and even the
exigencies of the law, are much more stringent
upon such points in Italy, than they are with us.
A nephew, who is capable of doing so, may be
compelled by law to support his uncle by the
father's side—(not so his mother's brother)—and
public opinion would extend the claims of kinship
very much further. To a mediæval Italian, it was
quite a matter of course that a brother, a son, a
father, or even a cousin, should suffer death for his
relative's political or other crime ; and this strong
solidarity of all the members of one house has left
deep traces in the manners and sentiments of the
people to the present day. Paolo Vanni may
have therefore felt, that he could not, without
risking a degree of opprobrium that he was not
prepared to face, refuse to take this little orphan
cousin, far away cousin though she was, to his
home.

But in the next place there are strong grounds
for thinking that Giulio Vanni, the father of little
Giulia, though a poor man, was not altogether a
destitute one. He must, people thought, have

left some little property behind him. But Paolo
Vanni, who was with him during his last illness
and at the time of his death, and who naturally
had the management of whatever small matters
there were to manage, showed that, when all was
paid, there was nothing left; that Giulia was
wholly unprovided for; that there was nothing
for it but for him to show his charity by supporting and bringing her up. I believe that if all
the yarn those rosy taper fingers had twiddled
off that eternal distaff had been fairly sold in
Ancona, the proceeds would have paid the cost of
Giulia's keep. I have a strong idea, too,—to speak
out plainly, and shame that old thief against
whose machinations Paolo Vanni was always paying insurance money,—that if that troublesome
voice, which has been mentioned as bothering the
wealthy farmer, could have been overheard, one
might have learnt some curious particulars about
the executorship accounts of Giulio Vanni. Don
Evandro, at all events, must have known all about
it . . . . *sub sigillo confessionis* . . . . for Paolo
was a very religious man.

All these matters, however, were bygones, and
altogether beside the present purpose. Whether
Giulia Vanni had ever been entitled to any

modicum of this world's goods or not, she clearly possessed none *now*,—at the time, that is, to which the singular events to be related in the following pages refer,—some year or so before the present time of writing. It will be more to the purpose to tell the reader what Giulia at that time *had*.

She had eighteen years; and all the knowledge, experience, wisdom, health, and talents that could be gathered in that space of time on the slope of an Apennine valley; and not altogether such a bad dower either, as some of the more tocher'd lasses of the cities either on the northern or the southern side of the Alps may perhaps be disposed to imagine. Imprimis, there was a figure five feet seven inches in height; lithe, springy, light, agile as that of a mountain goat; a step like a fawn's, and a carriage of the pretty small head to match; a fair broad brow, not very lofty, but giving unmistakable promise of energy of character and good practical working intelligence; above it a wonderful profusion of raven black hair, not very fine, but glossy as the raven's wing, and falling on either side from the parting at the top of the head in natural ripples, on which the sunbeams played in a thousand

hide-and-seek effects of light and shade ; well-
opened large black eyes, frank and courageous,
with a whole legion of wicked laughing imps
dancing and flashing about like fire-flies in the
depths of them ; a little delicately formed *nez
retroussé*, which very plainly said "beware" to
such as had the gift of interpreting nature's code
of signals ; a large but exquisitely formed mouth,
the favourite trysting-place of smiles and innocent
waggeries, the home of irresistible sweetness,—a
mouth that bade him, or even her, who looked
on it pay no heed to the warning conveyed by
neighbour nose, but, on the contrary, place boundless trust and confidence in the proprietress of it,
—a mouth whose signals every human thing with
eyes in its head could read, whereas only cyni-
cally philosophic physiognomists, who had burned
their fingers, or at least their hearts, by former
investigations of similar phenomena, could understand what that queer little nose said. It cannot
perhaps be fairly asserted that all these good
things were wholly the gift of old Apennine ; but
the splendid colouring,—a study for Giorgione!—
the rich, clear brown cheek, with a hue of the
sun's own painting, like that which he puts, when
he most delicately touches it, on an October

peach !—that was Apennine's own present to his
daughter! For the rest, the mountain women
said that Giulia Vanni was too slight to be good
for anything—a mere wisp! The mountain men
said that she was as beautifully made as any
lady of the cities. The town women said that
her waist was thick and clumsy. The town men,
when they saw her, thought slender waists a
mistake. Phidias would have said that she was
the incarnation of his beau idéal.

In short, no lovelier nut-brown maid ever stepped
a hillside than Giulia Vanni, as she was at eighteen
years of age! That warning nose might hang out
what signals it pleased, and that host of laughing
devils in her eyes might mockingly bid you take
care, every time your glance met hers ;—it was all
in vain! The male creature under thirty that
looked on Giulia Vanni fell in love with her!
And how well she knew her power! And how
she enjoyed her royalty ! And what pleasant fun
she found it to scatter her fire-darts around, herself scatheless and invulnerable the while, the
cruel Diana that she was !

But if it was impossible to look on the brilliant,
flashing, dangerous creature for an instant without
receiving a wound from her eyes, what must have

been the lot of poor Beppo Vanni, the eldest of
Sunta's two sons! Poor Beppo, who had to live in
the same house with her, to grow up with her, to
share his work with her, to play with her, and
laugh with her, to have little household secrets
with her, to be her slave and work for wages in
smiles not unpunctually paid—what could become
of him? What, but to worship the very ground
she trod on, and look to the hope of winning her
as the lode-star of his life!

Winning her, quotha!—a pretty winning, old
Paolo and old Sunta considered it! *Winning* a
wife without so much as a pearl necklace to begin
the world with! And he, Beppo Vanni, heir to
the lease of Bella Luce and—nobody knew, not
even dame Sunta—how many thousands of *scudi*
besides. Not if they knew it! The sly puss
might see what she could win for herself; but it
would not be Beppo Vanni—no, nor even Carlo
Vanni, his younger brother.

And thus it appears what else there was,
besides those suspected small-voiced importunities
which have been hinted at, to make old Paolo
Vanni querulous and discontented. Besides, it was
not only that his son and heir was bent on making
a fool of himself by marrying a girl without a

bajocco; but he would not make a match which
his father was very anxious to secure for him.
Don Evandro, like a true friend of the family, had
proposed the thing in the first instance, and would
doubtless have managed the whole affair with that
tact and success which the Italian clergy are so
remarkable for in such matters, if only Beppo
would have been reasonable. But to his father's
intense annoyance, he would not; having been
bewitched and rendered wholly unreasonable
by the "laughing devils" in Giulia's eyes. Don
Evandro had tried to exorcise them once, sum-
moning Giulia to an interview in the sacristy for
that purpose. But it was clear from the result
that he did not succeed; and he never tried a
second time!

To Beppo himself it was really a question—
could he win her ? And a very dubious question
too. It was not that he was not perfectly well
aware of the advantages of his social position. He
knew all that was due to the presumed future
tenant of Bella Luce. He knew that his father
was the richest man in the parish of Santa Lucia,
and in the neighbouring parishes around it
(putting the owners of the soil who lived in the
cities, and of whom the cultivators of the soil saw

little, out of the question ; as of course they *were* out of the question) ; he knew that he was presumably his father's heir ; and he was quite as well aware as any Romagnole peasant of the value of money and the social position it commands—which is equivalent to saying, he was as well aware as anybody in the world. But for all that it was an anxious question with him—could he hope to win her ? He knew that she had absolutely nothing ; that she was maintained by his father's charity ; and for all that it was with him a very anxious question, whether he could win Giulia Vanni for his wife or no.

And Giulia herself ? What was her view of the matter ? Her public conduct in the little world of Bella Luce, and her private feeling ? Well, the last perhaps is hardly a fair question. Perhaps Giulia would herself scarcely have been able to answer it consistently and entirely, even if her own heart were the asker. I suspect that her own heart never had categorically asked of her that question up to the time in question. Of course the writer has a means of forming some notion as to the real state of her feelings at that period—a clearer one perhaps than she could have formed herself—because he has the know-

ledge of her subsequent conduct to guide him to
an appreciation of them. And it will probably be
best to let the reader arrive at a knowledge of
the secrets of her inmost heart in the same
manner. As to her visible behaviour in the little
Bella Luce world, little, it must be admitted, can
be said in defence of it, beyond what Beppo
always said, appearing to consider that it was
an abundantly ample answer to all possible fault-
finding.

"But she is so beautiful!" he would say;
"she is *so* beautiful!"

So she was! But that did not justify her in
wearing an honest man's heart to fiddle-strings!
spoiling his rest, destroying his appetite for
supper, and keeping him awake o' nights. And
really, if it had been the settled purpose of her
life to do all these cruel things, she could not
have set about it in a more workwoman-like
manner. Did you ever observe a kitten rub its
nose and cheek against a person's hand, purring
in the most insinuatingly flattering manner all
the while, and then start away with a sudden
bound, rush under a neighbouring chair, and then
put up its little back and spit? Well, this was
exactly the type of Giulia's manner to Beppo!

There was never anything of *tenderness*,—no
symptom of love,—such love as Beppo wanted,—
to be detected in her manner, in her looks, in
the tone of her voice. But she would be so
good, so kind, so frankly affectionate, that he
would be tempted either by eye or voice to
some manifestation of the passion that was consuming him. No sooner had he done so than
she was off like a startled fawn, and either avoided
him, or was cross to him for the rest of the day.

There was one sign only that might perhaps
have led an intelligent looker-on at the game to
hope that there might be something better in
store for poor Beppo, though it altogether failed
to assure or comfort him. This was the way in
which Giulia would behave when others attacked,
or slighted, or belittled Beppo ; especially when
his brother, who was about two years his junior,
and just Giulia's own age, did so, as was not
unfrequently the case. Then, indeed, it was
clear enough that Beppo had a *friend*, if nothing else, in his beautiful cousin ! And surely
it ought to have led him to see a thing or two!
Only Beppo was not the man to see anything
that anybody tried to hide from him. Besides,
it was more generally in his absence that Giulia

would make a sortie, like a tigress from a jungle in defence of her young, in Beppo's behalf. And Carlo would get a scratch from the claw that he did not forget as soon as he ought to have done. And then old Paolo or dame Sunta would sneer and say something disagreeable if they were present ; and Giulia would be as cross and scratchy as possible to Beppo afterwards.

This younger brother Carlo was by no means a lad of whose allegiance most pretty girls would have been otherwise than proud. He was, though not so tall as his brother, who was slightly taller than his father,—and *he* was over six feet in his stockings,—nevertheless, like most of the Romagnole peasantry, a very fine young man. He was of a lighter build altogether than his brother, somewhat darker in hair and eyes, and of a less jovially ruddy brown complexion. Beppo would have been deemed probably the handsomer specimen of manhood by a jury of girls—(delivering a secret verdict to a female judge)—taken from the fields and hill-sides. Carlo might perhaps have had the verdict from a similar jury chosen from a city population. Then he was cleverer than Beppo, or at least was held to be so by all the world in which they both lived, including Don

Evandro, and both Beppo and Carlo themselves.
Beppo considered Carlo as a quite unprecedented
(at least in those parts) prodigy of genius. And
Carlo, if not quite persuaded of the justice of
that opinion, was thoroughly convinced that his
brother was a brainless lout, while he himself
was a very clever fellow.

He was the cleverer of the two certainly. His
intelligence was the readier and nimbler. He
was the better scholar, wrote a better hand, and
was infinitely quicker at accounts, or calculations.
But Beppo, though slow, was no fool; and there
are many subjects—and those not amongst the
least important that human hearts and heads are
called upon to decide for themselves—respecting
which—give him time to bring his mind to bear
upon the point—I would far rather have bound
myself to be ruled by Beppo's than by Carlo's
judgment. And then one was always sure to
know what Beppo really did think and feel.
And I am not so clear of that in the case of
master Carlo.

Perhaps old Paolo and Sunta might have made
up their minds to allow young Carlo and Giulia to
come together if only she would have kept her
hands off the sacred person of Beppo their first-

born. It is too bad to use such language! As if
Giulia showed any sign of wanting to I
think I can see how her eye would flash, and all
those laughing devils in it we talked of would
turn to fire-darting furies, if the phrase were used
in her presence. But that was the thought of
the old couple upon the subject. And though
I don't think either of them would have dared
to say as much in crude words in Giulia's hearing, I have little doubt that she had to brook
many a sneer and insinuation of the sort from
them,—to be rebutted by cruel treatment from
her towards poor Beppo, and, I strongly suspect,
to be followed by midnight hours of weeping,
and bursts of passionate agony, of which laughing, flashing, proud, scornful Giulia's pillow was
the only witness.

I think, as has been said, that Giulia might
have had Carlo Vanni if she would. But though
there were symptoms enough that he would have
been well pleased to settle all the family disagree-
ments in that manner, it was very clear that
Giulia would have nothing to say to any such
arrangement.

Clever, sharp Carlo, with his handsome dark
eye, his locks as black as her own, his fine long

Grecian nose, and light *svelte* figure, did not suit her taste. Was it really true that she liked heavy, good-natured Beppo, with his honest dark-blue eyes, and curly dark-brown hair, and Herculean shoulders, at all better? Old Paolo would have sneered bitterly in reply, that Giulia knew which side of the bread the butter was, none better! Young Beppo would have almost as bitterly answered, that she cared as much about him as she did about the oxen in the stable!

In fact, he often did say so; for it was a favourite comparison of himself in poor Beppo's mouth.

"I don't remember ever to have seen cousin Giulia steal away into the fields to help the oxen at their work, the way she went off t'other night to help you, Beppo, with shucking that lot of *gran-turco** in the loft," said Carlo once, viciously, for his father and mother were present.

"Because the *gran-turco* would never have been finished that night, if I hadn't given a hand; for Beppo was so sleepy he could not hold his stupid head up!" replied Giulia, colouring up and tossing her head.

* The common country name for maize in Italy—"Turkish grain."

"And wouldn't she do as much or more for you, or for *Babbo*,* or for old Cecco, the blind beggarman, or for the oxen either, for that matter? Would not she do anything on earth she could for any living creature?" demanded Beppo, with immense energy. "But for me more than another," he added, with bitterness, "no! You know better than that, Carlo!"

But what would most have tended to make all straight and comfortable at Bella Luce, would have been that Beppo should have made up his mind to the match which his father and his parish priest had picked out for him. And there was really very little reason why he should not do so; —very little reason, that is to say, except those mischief-making eyes of cousin Giulia;—and the natural and notorious perversity of Dan Cupid, who really can only be led or driven by parents and guardians on the same principle on which Paddy is said to have succeeded in driving his pig from Cork to Dublin,—"by making the cratur think it's from Dublin to Cork that I'm wanting him to go!"

If cousin Giulia had been out of the question, really Beppo might have done worse than make

---

* Daddy, the common phrase with Italians of all classes.

up to Lisa Bartoldi, the rich Fano attorney's only daughter ; as his father, and Don Evandro, and Lisa's father, old Sandro Bartoldi, wished him to do.

Ay, if cousin Giulia were out of the question ! as she would have been if Paolo Vanni had never taken her to live at Bella Luce.

" See what comes of doing a charitable action, and sacrificing one's own interest to one's good- ness of heart ! It's always the way !" said old Paolo Vanni one day, in talking the grievance over with his guide, philosopher, and friend, Don Evandro.

The priest did not answer him save by a steady and meaning look right into the old man's eyes ; the full translation and meaning of which I take to have been, that that able divine and confessor wished to intimate that his view of the circum- stances in question placed that bringing home of the orphan cousin on the debtor, and not at all on the creditor, side of that double-entry account between his parishioner and the Recording Angel, which it was his duty to keep properly posted up.

And, after all, it was not so clear that all would have gone upon wheels—as the Italian phrase has it—even if cousin Giulia had never come to Bella

Luce. Beppo might possibly have looked kindly
on Lisa. But the attorney's daughter was not a
bit more disposed to accept Beppo Vanni for a
husband than he was to take her to wife. And
that, at all events, was not cousin Giulia's fault!
And though old Sandro Bartoldi was very desirous
that his daughter should marry all Paolo Vanni's
hoarded scudi, he was far too doting a father to
his motherless girl to have attempted compulsion.

And really Lisa Bartoldi was a very nice girl,—
pretty, delicate-featured, golden-haired, blue-eyed,
very fragile-looking, and slender. Worse wrong
could not have been done her than to place her
side by side with Giulia Vanni. It was to make
her appear a poor, washed-out, faded, half-alive
wisp of a creature by contrast with that richly
developed and magnificent organisation! Her
hair was really golden when the sun lent a little
real golden light to tinge it. Her complexion
was really charmingly delicate, with the faintest
possible tint of the blush-rose in the cheek. But
by the side of Giulia she seemed to fade into a
general whity-brown atony of colour, like wood-
ashes that still glow feebly in the gloom, but fade
into lightless grey when the sun's beam touches

them. "*Che vuole!*"* as the gossips said. Poor
Lisa had been born and had grown up in a very
dull house, in a very dull street, in the very dull
town of Fano, while Giulia had been drinking,
from morning to night, the free, fresh air of the
breezy Apennine. What chance had Lisa in
sleepy, stuffy Fano, from which even the sea-
breeze is shut out by its walls, and by a range of
sand-hills still higher than they, with a creep to
mass in a neighbouring church for her whole dis-
sipation, and a crawl on the *passeggiata*† under
the lime-trees on festa days for her sole exercise ?

Lisa knew, however, a great many things that
Giulia did not ;—necessarily so. Not that, to the
best of my judgment, she was in any degree the
cleverer girl, or had the more powerful intellect of
the two. In the first place, I have a great notion
of the truth of the *mens sana in corpore sano ;*
and, in the next place, there was always a sort of
feeble, sickly sentimentalism—a great deal more
common on the northern than on the southern
side of the Alps—about Lisa, which did not give
me the idea of a strongly-constituted mind. But,
of course, she was by far the more cultivated, had

* "What would you have ?" or, "What can you expect ?"
† Parade, town-walk.

far more pretention to lady-like manners —
(though it must be understood that there is infinitely less difference in this respect between one
woman and another in Italy than among ourselves,
the manners of the lower classes being better, and
those of the upper strata of society worse, or at
least less refined, less educated, and less con-
ventional, than those of the corresponding classes
at home)—and to refinement. Though, as to
lady-like feeling, my own impression is, that
Giulia's sentiments, if one could have got at her
heart and seen them there *in situ*, instead of
coming at them through the medium of her own
exposition of them, would be found to be such as
might have done honour to any crusader-descended
duchess, and set a very useful example to not a
few such.

And Lisa Bartoldi was a good girl in her way,
too. But dull, Herculean Beppo, with the frank,
deep blue, steadfast eyes, and the honest, sunburnt, open face, would have nothing to say to
her, preferring his nature-created duchess. Not
that it ever had entered into his head to compare
the two. Compare our Giulia to Lisa Bartoldi!
or, indeed, to any other of mortal mould!!

No; he *could* have nothing to say to Lisa—

nothing to say to her, that is, in the way of love, for they were very good friends, perfectly understood one another, and sympathised upon the subject, and would speak very freely upon it when they met, as was often the case, on occasion of the young farmer of Bella Luce coming into Fano on market-days.

And indeed they found much to say to each other upon such occasions. For Lisa had a secret of her own—a secret the joint property of herself and a certain captain of Bersaglieri,* one Giacopo Brilli—which she had no objection to trust to great, honest Beppo, in return for his bewailments of his hapless passion. The exchange was hardly a fair one; for Lisa was happy in her love, and, with a little perseverance, had not much to fear from the rigour of a doting father, who, however, for the present, declared that it was altogether impossible to bestow his heiress daughter on a man who proposed " no consideration, positively none !" in return. It would be a one-sided and altogether unformal contract. Besides, it was no secret that simple Beppo gave in return for Lisa's confidences. All the world knew his pains ! He would bellow out his soft complainings to any one

* The Rifle Corps.

E 2

who would listen to him, pouring out all his great, big, earnest, simple, deeply-smitten heart.

Carlo said once that Beppo reminded him, when the elegiac fit was on him, of one of his own oxen, breathing with outstretched head its melancholy bellowings to the breeze as it went a-field. And if Giulia's eyes could have wielded daggers as well as look them, when he so spoke, methinks Carlo would never have jibed at his brother or any one else any more.

Farmer Paolo Vanni, and his counsellor Don Evandro, supposing it finally admitted that it was beyond their united power to bring Beppo and Lisa together, would have been glad to secure the Fano attorney's crowns on behalf of his younger brother, Carlo. And Carlo, despite a certain degree of inclination to make love to his beautiful cousin, half due to real admiration of her beauty, and half to a feeling that it would be very pleasant to carry her off from under his brother's nose, would have had no difficulty in acceding to such an arrangement. But neither in this way did it seem likely, for the reasons that the reader is in possession of, that Sandro Bartoldi's money could be made available for increasing the greatness of the Bella Luce family.

And it is now intelligible, also, why old Paolo Vanni, despite all his worldly prosperity, was not altogether a happy man, and why the Bella Luce household was not an abode of that unbroken felicity, contentment, and peace of mind, which are usually supposed to be the characteristics of dwellings placed in romantic situations, and ten miles from the nearest post-office.

CHAPTER IV.

HE seniors of the party, whose comfortable and reasonable arrangements were all thus disturbed and traversed by Dan Cupid's tricksy perversities and self-willed rebelliousness, were not, however disposed to give up the game without some further attempt at winning it. And matters stood at Bella Luce as has been indicated in the preceding chapter, when shrewd old Sandro Bartoldi, the rich Fano attorney, made a move with a view of weakening the enemy by a diversion. Intent on a scheme he had concocted with this purpose, the attorney ordered his stout, well-fed cob, one fine March morning, for a ride up to Bella Luce. Neither Sandro nor his beast were so well inclined to active movement as they once had been. They took the uphill work easily,

therefore, among the lanes that crept up the green valleys; and, though they left Fano betimes in the morning, only reached their destination some half an hour before noon.

That, indeed, was the hour at which the attorney had wished to time his arrival. For his errand required that he should hold a conference with the head of the Bella Luce family; and he knew very well that on this precious bright March morning all the males of the place would be at their avocations in the fields. But at noon came the hour of repose, and of the mid-day meal—the hours, rather, for few labourers, either in city or in country, of whatever class, allow themselves or are allowed by their employers less than two hours—from twelve till two.

March is a busy month in the country in Italy. It is the time for pruning and dressing the vines. And it was on this work that old Paolo Vanni and his two sons were engaged when Sandro Bartoldi rode up the last steep bit of the hollow lane that climbed from the bottom of the valley to the level of the house.

A French vineyard is one of the ugliest agricultural sights in nature. Nothing can be more unsightly than little low bushes, not much bigger

than uggly brown cabbages, set in rows along the
fields. But France produces good wine, and de-
clares that this is the only way to do so. For the
present, however, Italy is content to drink her
somewhat harsher and coarser, but more generous,
wines, and to hold to the picturesque old method
of cultivation that Virgil has described. Paolo,
Beppo, and Carlo Vanni were tending their vines
exactly as any Corydon, or Tityrus, or Thyrsis did
two thousand years ago on the same hill-sides—
marrying them with wedding-knots of withy, not
exactly to elms, but to the white mulberry trees.
These also had been previously pruned, and the
wood and the leaves carefully gathered, till little
remained save the trunks, whose office was to
support the vines, and a few leading branches
cut into a cup-shaped form at the top of the
trunk, destined to produce a fresh crop of shoots
and leaves from the old, much-scarred, pollard
head.

The rich, red tilled land of the large field in
which they were all three at work, was now nearly
covered with the bright green of the young crop.
For the Italian agriculturist, unlike the French,
does not think that his field has done enough when
it has given him wine; the same land must give

its corn, too; and, generally, to make up the Scriptural trio, its oil also.

The father and the two sons were in different parts of the field, at some distance from each other, each engaged on a separate tree. They were all mounted on broad double ladders, some five feet wide at the base, tapering as they rose to a height of about twelve feet or so from the ground, to a width of six or eight inches, and ending in a little platform of those dimensions. The old man was in his shirt-sleeves, and wore short fustian knee-breeches, and bright blue worsted stockings. The two young men wore trousers of cloth; for Bella Luce was not utterly beyond the limits of fashion's jurisdiction; though her writs were made returnable thence a considerable time after they were issued. Beppo and Carlo Vanni also had retained their jackets, either in consequence of a falling off from the hardiness of the previous generation, or from a sentiment of respect for the presence of the lovely Giulia. Each of the three had a peculiarly shaped small hatchet suspended, save at the moments when it was in use, by a hook at the end of its handle, from a strap around his loins, and a bundle of slender osier twigs tied in front of his shoulders;

—the first to do the pruning; the second for the
tying of that Virgilian marriage-knot which was
to unite the drooping vine firmly to its support
till after the vintage.

Giulia was in the field, as has been intimated,
and was busy in gathering and binding into
bundles the prunings, to be carefully carried to
the homestead as precious food for the sheep and
goats. This duty required her presence under the
different trees on which the three men were engaged, one after the other; and Giulia was very
careful to linger no longer over her work under
the one tree than under the other. What! give
old Paolo an opportunity of grumbling, or Carlo a
chance of sneering, that she sought to make time
for saying a few *tête-à-tête* words to poor Beppo!
Not if she were never to have the chance of saying
another!

Perhaps ball-room belles fancy that only their
lot subjects them to the delicate embarrassments
of similar considerations, and that the "happy
simplicity of the peasant's life" frees them from
all such little troubles. Ah! Giulia Vanni in
the upland farm of Bella Luce could have told
them a different story!

However, be scrupulous as she might to gather

the vine cuttings under each plant as quickly as she could, and to linger no longer over one part of her work than another, it was impossible to avoid giving each of the three men, in turn, an opportunity of saying a few words to her from the top of his ladder, which was out of earshot of the others.

The field in which the party was at work commanded the hollow lane by which the Fano attorney was approaching Bella Luce; and it so happened that Giulia, who was at that moment gathering up Beppo's cuttings, was the first to catch sight of the guest.

"Beppo! there is a man on horseback coming up the lane! I declare I think . . . . yes, it certainly is," she added, shading her eyes with her hand, "old Sandro, the attorney at Fano!"

"What can he be coming here for? . . . . no good, you may swear!" said Beppo, who considered the attorney only in the light of one of a conspiracy to deprive him of Giulia.

"Fie, Beppo! I am sure you ought not to say that of him, of all people in the world! As if you did not know that he was coming here to propose his daughter for your excellency's acceptance!"

"The apoplexy catch him and his daughter,

too! No, poor Lisa! I don't mean that! But
I wish he would let Lisa go her way, and me
mine!"

"What a fine thing it must be to be a rich
signore, and to have the girls, pretty ones, too,
like Lisa, coming to beg for the honour of your
alliance! But it's cruel to be hard upon her,
Beppo! I would not refuse her, for we poor girls,
you know, are apt to break our silly hearts for
you ungrateful men."

"Giulia! how can you go on so? As if you
did not know! Ah! it's only the girls who
break their hearts, I suppose. Well! if you don't
know—"

"All I know is, that I must run and tell the
padrone"—it was so that Giulia always spoke of
the master of the family;—"that Ser Sandro is
coming up the hill! Good-bye, Beppo! Don't be
cruel to poor Lisa!"

And off she tripped to the part of the field
where Paolo was at work, and from which that
part of the hollow lane in which the attorney was
riding was not visible.

"'Gnor padrone! There is Ser Sandro, from
Fano, coming up the hill! Had I not better run
and tell the *padrona?*"

" Ser Sandro coming ? where ? "

" He is in the hollow of the lane there ; I saw him just now."

" Whatever is in the wind to bring him out to Bella Luce to-day of all days in the year ! " exclaimed old Paolo. " Yes, run, my girl, run, and tell *la sposa* that Ser Sandro will take a mouthful of dinner with us ! "

Giulia waited for no second bidding, but ran off to the house, to prepare the mistress for the great and unusual event which was impending over Bella Luce, while old Paolo came down from his ladder, and, with his pruning-hatchet still hanging at his loins behind, and his bundle of withy twigs still stuck in front of him, hastened to the edge of the field where it overlooked the hollow way, to greet his visitor as he came up.

" Why, Signor Sandro ! " he said from the top of the bank, as the attorney passed below him, " who would have thought of seeing you out at Bella Luce this morning ! What news from town ? How is the Signora Lisa ? Come up, come up ! there'll be a mouthful of something or another to eat in the house."

" Eat ! Ah ; you may talk about eating up here ! What a beautiful air you have on the

hill-side here. Per bacco, life must be worth fifty
per cent. longer purchase here than down in the
city there ! "

" What time did you start this morning, Signor
Sandro ? "

" Oh, we've taken it easy, Moro and I! I
knew there was no use in getting here before
the *angelus*, if I wanted to speak with you, Signor
Paolo ! How are the vines looking ? "

" There is not much to boast of ! If we have a
glass of wine to drink, it is as much as we shall
have ! "

" Why, they tell me that there are no signs of
the disease yet, none even down in the plains ;
and you are sure to be better off here ! "

" Wait a bit ! It's too soon yet ! You'll see
in another couple of months ! I never cry till
I'm out of the wood. The disease will come quite
time enough, never you fear ! What else can you
expect ? "

" Expect ! why should I expect it ? There was
much less of it last year than the year before ! I
expect to have none this year ! "

" And do you think that is likely, Signor
Sandro, with such maledictions as we have in
these blessed times ! With the beastly smoking,

spluttering railway, that's going to be finished
they say this year, is it likely that the air would
not be poisoned ? There'll be no more crops such
as there used to be,—you mark my words!—as
long as those things are in the country. Why, it
stands to reason, they are against nature ! "

"I know there are many that consider the vine
disease to be caused by the railroad," replied
Signor Sandro ; " very good judges and competent
persons too, ay, and 'sponsible men like yourself,
Signor Paolo. So I'm sure it's not for me to say
it is not so. Only they do say that the disease
is just the same, where there are no railroads."

Chatting thus, the attorney and the farmer
approached the house and each other together—
the former coming up the road which reached the
level of the house and of the field, along the edge
of which the latter was walking a few yards only
from the door.

Beppo and Carlo had come down from their
pruning ladders, and were following their father
at some distance towards the house.

Giulia meanwhile, after communicating her
tidings to Signora Sunta, slipped away to her
own chamber to make some little preparation for
appearing before the eyes of the townsman. She

would not have dreamed of doing anything of the
sort for any visitors from any of the neighbouring
farms or villages, young or old, male or female.
But the Italian peasant has, without much—at all
events acknowledged—respect or liking for the
city or its inhabitants, a very great awe and
admiration for the townsfolk. The peasant con-
siders them to be less honest, less kind, less
hearty and healthy, less instructed in all matters
really worth knowing, than he himself is. At all
events he professes so to consider. But he looks
upon the luxury, the taste, the pomp, the magnificence, and the finery of the neighbouring city,
as something wonderful and stupendous ;—affects
to reprobate and despise it all, and probably, if
an old man, would in reality not change his own
life for a city one ; but nevertheless looks up to
his town-bred neighbours with a very considerable
sense of their superior position.

This same feeling, which had sent Giulia off in
a hurry to her chamber, manifested itself in *la
sposa* in care for the reputation of her kitchen.
It was supremely displeasing to her that a stranger
from the city should arrive thus unannounced a
few minutes only before the dinner hour. If she
could have got warning in time, she would have

sent into Fano for delicacies of all sorts. If there
was no time for that, she would have ransacked
the neighbouring villages. But here she was left
to make the best figure she could entirely on her
own resources. And she had no doubt that the
townsman thus managed that his visit should be
wholly unannounced, for the express purpose of
triumphing over her unprovidedness. That he
might himself be hungry and like a good dinner,
and be pleased at getting one at Bella Luce, never
occurred to her as a possible phase of the matter.
It shaped itself to her mind as a contest between
town and country, in which the townsman's object would be attained, and his vanity gratified at
the expense of hers, in proportion to the poor-
ness of the fare set before him. For to an
Italian the gratification of an appetite is a small
matter in comparison with the gratification of a
vanity.

So *la sposa*, much and deeply grumbling between
her teeth, set herself to do all that could be done
at so short a notice.

"Carlo," she said to her second son, as he came
in from the field, "run quick to his reverence, and
tell him to come and take a bit of dinner with us,
and ask *la* Nunziata (the priest's housekeeper) to

send me a pot of her quince preserve, and some biscuits,—quick."

It must not be supposed that the priest was invited for the sake of the quince sweetmeats and the biscuits. He and they were equally benefactions to her board, and the priest himself by far the most important of the two. It was respectable and in good style, and perhaps even what Signor Sandro himself could not have accomplished at so short a notice, to have the parish priest at the board. His reverence, on his part, it may be observed, hastened to put on his very best coat and a clean collar, not so much from any personal care about, or vanity in such matters, but in order to do honour to Signor Vanni's board, and to support the country in its contest with the city. That was the feeling of the priest, as it would also have been of any of the neighbours. They were all in one boat, so far as the necessity for hiding the nakedness of their land, and making the best possible appearance in the eyes of the townsman went.

Meanwhile Sunta did her utmost within the cruelly short space of time which the cunning of the citizen had allowed her. Eggs in abundance were brought in from the poultry-house and

stables, and *la sposa* proceeded to concoct a
frittata with slices of ham cunningly introduced
into a stratified formation of egg and flour, fried
in abundance of oil, and flavoured with some herbs,
according to a special receipt in the possession of
Signora Sunta, and which were supposed to be
Apennine products unobtainable in the towns.
Beppo was sent to catch and kill a fowl in all
haste, and prepare it for instant spitch-cocking.
This, with a sweet confection, in which more eggs
were the principal ingredient, and the *minestra*—
the pottage—which would have constituted the
entire dinner for the family, if Signor Sandro had
stayed at home, made out a tolerably presentable
repast, especially when accompanied by an un-
stinted supply of Signor Vanni's choicest wine,
which they all knew was really such as the
attorney did not drink every day of his life.

But for all this, be it observed, the Bella Luce
family, however anxious to shine in the eyes of
their guest, did *not* dream of changing the venue
of their repast to the great eating-room up-stairs.
That would have been too serious and solemn an
affair to be thought of for such a mere extemporary
matter as the present. The dinners eaten in that
state-room *were* dinners indeed ! To have placed

the hurriedly prepared modest meal of to-day
before their guest in that huge, bare-looking
guest-chamber, would have been to render it and
themselves ridiculous.   So the little party sat
down as usual at the table in the kitchen, which
was the common living-room of the family.

Giulia stole down from her room, the young
men washed their hands and faces, the anxious
and hard-working Sunta seized a moment to give
one re-ordering touch to her hair and kerchief
after her culinary labours, and then announced
to her husband, and Don Evandro and Signor
Sandro Bartoldi, that " their lordships were served,"
i. e., in base plebeian terms, that the dinner was
ready.

" It's not to be expected," said Signora Sunta,
as they sate down, with an *aigre doux* manner,
half mock-modest hospitality, and half self-assert-
ing defiance, " that the like of us can set before a
gentleman from the city anything fit for him to
eat, and that too at a moment's notice ! I am afraid
the soup is not what you can eat, Signor Sandro !"

" On the contrary, my dear madam, I positively
must take the liberty of asking for another ladle-
ful.   I was just thinking that I had never tasted
a better *minestra* in my life !"

"Ay! that's our Bella Luce air! We can grow appetites up here, if our soil is too poor to grow anything else!" said farmer Paolo.

The farm of Bella Luce was anything but poor land; but an Italian farmer always calls his land poor, and a landowner as invariably deems it rich.

"Any way," said the priest, "I find that, let me bring what appetite I may to Bella Luce, I never take any away with me, and I dare say Signor Sandro will experience the same thing."

"That I'll be sworn I shall!" said the attorney.

"There's no dinner, to say dinner!" replied *la sposa*. "You are sadly out of luck to-day, Signor Sandro! This is such a place out here in the mountains. There's never a bit of meat to be got at Santa Lucia except Saturdays. There's nothing for your dinner except a grilled fowl of my own fattening, and a Bella Luce *frittata*, and some rashers of our own curing, and a bit of salad"—the lettuce had been brought by Don Evandro in his handkerchief from his own little bit of garden, and given privately to the *padrona* with many precautions against the detection of the transaction by the guest,—and a *dolce*, and some preserve, and a few biscuits!

"Oh! oh! oh! What a dinner! What a

feast!" exclaimed the attorney. "How you
country people do live! Ah, one must come into
the country to know what living means."

"But you are not to think, Signor Sandro, that
all my parishioners live as they do at Bella Luce,"
said the priest. "*Tutt' altro, lo posso dir io!* *
There's not such another farm as Bella Luce, and
not such another manager as *la* Signora Sunta, in
all the country-side."

"I believe you. Look at this cloth and these
napkins," rejoined the courtier-like attorney. "I
think I know whose hands spun the yarn; and I
think I could tell, if anybody in Fano asked me,
where to find enough of the same make to turn
all yonder cornfield as white as this table. Aha!
la sposa! Am I in the secret, eh? I think I
was honoured by a peep into the great press up-
stairs once upon a time; and *I* never saw such a
show, let the other be where it would!"

This touched the *corde sensible* in *la* Signora
Sunta's heart, and she was much flattered by
the compliment. She smirked and purred, and
admitted that, thank God! they were not badly
off for linen at Bella Luce; they had enough for
the needs of the house, and mayhap a trifle to

* Very much otherwise, I can assure you.

furnish forth a son's house at need—or maybe a couple of them for the matter of that!

And thereupon Beppo suddenly suspended half-way between the table and his open mouth the huge fragment of bread, with which he had been scouring his plate round and round, in order to mop up the last viscous particles of the *frittata*, and looked hard across the table at Giulia, blushing crimson the while all over his great frank face, as if the most excruciatingly delicate and suggestive thing had been uttered. Giulia, on her part, kept her eyes fixed on her plate, and would have been supposed by anybody, who had never had any daughter of Eve under his observation before, to have been wholly unaware of Beppo's demonstration.

"You don't drink, Signor Sandro! Yet the wine is not so bad as it might be, though I say it that should not," observed old Paolo.

"Per Bacco! I've drunk enough to find out that we town's-folk must not drink it without counting our glasses. *È un gran' vino, davvero! Che colore! Che squisito sapore! È fior di roba!*"* said the attorney, holding his glass up

---

* It's a grand wine, truly! What a colour! What exquisite flavour! It's a very choice article;—literally "flower of goods."

to the light. "We don't drink such wine down
in Fano, I can tell you, Signor Paolo !"

"And we don't make such at Bella Luce,
now-a-days;—more's the pity ! And never shall
again till these cursed railroads are cleared out
of the country . . . . and something else has
happened, that need not be more particularly
mentioned," said the old farmer.

Every one present knew very well that this
something else meant the restoration of the papal
government. And Signor Sandro Bartoldi thought
to himself, that if no more good wine was to
be made till that happened, it would be wise to
make the most of the old while it lasted. But
of course nobody was so un-Italianly imprudent
as to take any notice of the farmer's manifestation of his political faith. Don Evandro turned
up his eyes towards heaven, and took advantage
of the action to drain his glass; but no word
was said.

The railroad, however, was not a tabooed subject, and Beppo ventured, after mature consideration, to say that, if it was true, as he was told,
that the vine disease had visited countries where
there were no railroads, it did seem to him as if
they could not be the cause of it !"

"What has that to do with it, *figliuolo mio?*" cried the priest, firing up. "Do you think that the Almighty did not know that those countries were going to make those abominable things against nature, upsetting all society, and sent his curses for their punishment accordingly? Why, there is not one of those countries that you allude to that has not now, as I am informed, fallen into the iniquity. And are not the works of Providence thus justified, and is not the abomination of these nuisances proved past all denial?"

Beppo was too well brought up to dream of arguing with his parish priest. He made no reply; but set himself to consider the question, and soon arrived at the conclusion that he should like to ask Giulia what she thought about it?

Signor Sandro, protesting that he did not presume to judge the matter under its theological aspect, yet ventured to say that, in a wholly worldly point of view, he thought the railway was adding, and would add, to the riches of the country.

The priest answered him that all such wealth would be found to be of the nature of devil's money, and would turn to dust and ashes in the pockets of those who flattered themselves that they were enriched by it.

To this exposition of doctrine the attorney bowed meekly ; but thought to himself that, for all that, he should not part with a single one of the shares which were locked up in his strong box at home.

And so the dinner and the conversation went on till *la* Signora Sunta rose and left the table to prepare coffee for the three seniors of the party.

The two young men put cigars in their mouths and strolled out of the kitchen-door, Beppo giving a beseechingly inviting glance to Giulia to follow him as he went.

Giulia, however, was as blind to this appeal as she had been to the look across the dinner-table, and stealing out of the opposite door of the kitchen, which opened on the huge staircase, tripped up to the privacy of her own room.

CHAPTER V.

SIGNOR SANDRO BARTOLDI.

S SOON as the three seniors had been thus left to themselves, sitting over the table, at which they had been dining, and which continued covered with the cloth that had excited Ser Sandro's admiration, the attorney prepared to enter at once on the subject of his visit. The glasses and flasks were still upon the table; and the farmer and the priest replenished theirs yet once again; but the more abstemious townsman, less accustomed to deep potations, and who had been really in earnest when he said that Farmer Vanni's wine was of a quality that made it necessary to count the glasses, declined to drink any more, though strongly urged to do so by his two companions.

Signor Alessandro Bartoldi, the well-known

attorney of Fano, was a good sort of man enough
in his way. He had long been a widower, and
lived only for his one daughter. But he had very
little comprehension of living for her, or doing
anything for her, in any other way than by
increasing the handsome fortune which he had
already accumulated for her. Though too much
disposed to be all things to all men,—to be called
a perfectly honest man in the largest sense of the
word,—he was thoroughly such in the more
restricted and ordinarily understood signification
of the term. He was strictly honest in his pro-
fessional avocation, and in his pursuit of wealth ;
being genuinely persuaded that for that purpose,
at least in his department of the world's affairs,
honesty was the best policy. A veritable Vicar
of Bray in politics, he had quite sense enough
to understand that the recent changes were calculated to increase the material prosperity of
the country ; and was, therefore, well disposed
towards the new government. But, not being at
all of the stuff of which martyrs are made, he
had felt no disposition to risk getting himself
into trouble by taking any part in the extrusion
of the old order of things. He never talked politics, nor got into the way of hearing them talked

if he could help it. He always obeyed the law; and was one of those men who may take oaths of allegiance to a dozen different governments in succession, without being justly chargeable with any false swearing; for his allegiance was sincerely rendered to every ruler as long as he was in power; and he most assuredly never contemplated promising it for an hour longer. Besides, and after his daughter, the only thing he cared for in the world was his collection of ancient documents, charters,· grants, contracts, and such like, which was noted as the most important collection of the kind in that part of Italy, and by means of which he purposed some day illustrating a work on the history of Romagna and the March of Ancona.

He was a little, alert, brisk old gentleman, with a small, round, closely and always cleanly shaven face, a florid complexion, a shrewd twinkling eye, a benevolent expression of features, an almost entirely bald head, and a forehead deeply marked with a whole series of horizontal furrows, the result probably of a life-long habit of raising his eyebrows and assuming an expression intended to suggest that there was a great deal to be said on both sides, which he always resorted to whenever any difference of opinion or difficulty of any sort was mooted before him. If that little pantomime was found insufficient to set the matter at rest, as far as he was concerned, he would, if sitting down, nurse one leg laid over the knee of the other, handling it with the greatest tenderness, as if it represented the question in hand ; or, if standing up, stick his thumbs into the arm-holes of his waistcoat, throw his head back, and enunciate the ejaculation, " Per—r—r Bac—co ! " or, sometimes, if the case were a grave one, " Per—r—din—ci Bac—co ! " uttering the words very slowly and with a long-drawn breath, and following it up with three or four raisings and depressions of his chin, executed with a slow uniform motion like the working of a steam-engine piston.

Signor Alessandro Bartoldi was no fool withal ; but these little peculiarities constituted the arms, offensive and defensive, which he had found most available for making his way and holding his own in a somewhat disjointed world, and in difficult times.

" I wanted to speak to you to-day, my esteemed friend," said the attorney, addressing the farmer, " on a little matter, in which it has seemed to me that I might be able to be of use to you. I know

I may speak freely before his reverence ; for I am aware of the friendship that unites him to your family. Indeed, I am fortunate in having an opportunity of profiting by his valuable counsel in the matter;—though it is a bit of good fortune that I did not anticipate."

The priest gave a little bow, but said nothing. Signor Alessandro Bartoldi was no favourite of his; for Don Evandro was a politician of the class, whose members consider every one against them who is not with them ; and he knew what to expect from Sandro in that matter. Although the project of a marriage between Beppo Vanni and Lisa Bartoldi had been first set on foot by him, the idea had not arisen out of any personal intimacy between him and the attorney, but had first been suggested to him by a brother priest of Fano, who was anxious to secure the attorney's wealth to the good cause ; which Don Evandro had thought effectually to do by conferring it, with Lisa's hand, on the submissive son of his eminently right-minded parishioner and intimate friend, old Farmer Vanni.

Honest little Sandro, on the other hand, did not much like the priest, who had now and then a way of looking at him which he did not fancy.

He always felt in his company as if he were in
the presence of a sharp detective officer prepared
to make use against him of any word that might
fall from his lips should a time ever come when
the priest might find it desirable to do so. However, in obedience to his unfailing maxim and
practice to hold the best candle he could lay his
hands on to every devil or devil's emissary whom
he might be doomed to meet in his way through
life, he spoke as above in opening his business
with the farmer.

"Everybody knows," resumed the little man,
"the admirable and truly Christian manner in
·which you have received, educated, and supported
your orphan relative, the Signorina Giulia. All
Fano has rung with your praises on this score,
my valued friend, and you have well deserved
them !"

Don Evandro here looked at the farmer with
a fixed and peculiar look that caused the hard-
featured old man to drop his eyes before it. The
priest had no special reason for thus reminding
his parishioner of any circumstances that might
be in both their hearts at that moment. But it
was part of his system, so long practised as to
have become quite habitual to him, never to lose

any opportunity of acquiring or consolidating power over others, be they who they might, or let the means be what they might. That was all the object of the look—and the object was gained. The old man's eyes fell, and his heart recognised his master.

"But," resumed the attorney, "for a girl such as the Signorina Giulia, who has her bread to earn, and her way to make in the world, it would be a great thing to obtain some knowledge of many things which she would perhaps be more likely to pick up in the city than in your own undoubtedly more agreeable home. I put it to you, your reverence, since we are happy enough to have the benefit of your presence, whether it does not strike you in that like?"

"Most unquestionably!" replied the priest. "There can be no doubt about the matter. It would be extremely advantageous to *la* Giulia to sojourn for awhile in the city, if we only knew any means of placing her there with propriety. But that is the difficulty."

"Just so! that was the difficulty! Now that difficulty I think I have been fortunate enough to find the means of removing!"

"Indeed, Signor Sandro!" said Vanni, begin-

ning to see that the removal in question might be
desirable for more reasons than that assigned
by the cautious little attorney. "Truly we shall
have reason to be very much obliged to you.
What is it you are good enough to think of
proposing for *la* Giulia *poverina ?*"

"Why, this it is," replied Signor Sandro,
addressing himself to the farmer, but looking
at Don Evandro, and evidently considering him
as the more important personage to be consulted ;
"a friend and very good client of mine, an elderly
widow lady, whose—a—companion has lately left
her, wants to meet with—what shall I say ? Not
exactly a servant, and perhaps not altogether a
companion ; somebody, in short, who for a moderate recompense—moderate, for my friend is not
rich—would live with her, and take care of her
and her house, and be taught all of housekeeping
that my friend could teach—not a small matter,
allow me to say, for *la* Signora Clementina Dossi
is a capital housekeeper, I can tell you—and—do
what there is to be done in the house."   .

"Be a servant-of-all-work, in short !" said
Farmer Vanni.

"*Che ! che ! che !* Servant-of-all-work !" cried
the attorney, who had been particularly labouring

to prevent his proposition from assuming any such appearance; for he well knew and understood the *contadino* pride, which would be likely to rise in arms against such a proposal. It was not, as the attorney knew perfectly well, any tenderness on the part of the old farmer for his adopted child that made the notion of accepting a place as maid-of-all-work distasteful to him, but that he shrank from having it said that an inmate of Bella Luce, one of his family, and bearing his name, had been obliged to accept such a position.

"Nothing like a servant-of-all-work! scarcely a servant at all, I tell you."

"I should not like Giulia to take a place of maid-of-all-work. None of the Vannis have ever been in service!" said the old farmer, rather grimly.

"Of course not, my dear friend! Can you imagine such a thing? I should not like to stand in the shoes of the man who should come up to Bella Luce to propose to the head of the Vanni family to send one of its members to menial service. But this is quite a different matter. We are upon quite other ground. I appeal to his reverence here, whose opinion we should both

of us bow to implicitly, whether there is any
similitude between the two cases."

And Signor Sandro ventured a speaking look at
the priest as he spoke.

"Certainly it does seem to me," said the priest,
"since you ask my opinion, that this is a proposition which any man might freely accept without
in any degree compromising the credit of his
family. Judging, my dear Signor Vanni, from
the details Signor Sandro has been good enough
to lay before us, I should say that there was
nothing in common between the position he has
in view for the Signorina Giulia and that of a
menial servant."

"Clearly not! I was sure his reverence's
admirable judgment would see the thing in its
true light at once. You see, my dear friend,
there is no question of any wages as such;—
merely a gratuitous douceur, — '_gratitudinis
causa_,' I may say,—our friend Don Evandro will
appreciate the appropriateness of the expression;
—for service willingly rendered on the one hand,
and thankfully received, rather than exacted, on
the other. You will perceive, my esteemed Signor
Vanni, all the essential differences of the position
from that of one holding a menial capacity."

The farmer would have been very much puzzled to explain in what the difference consisted, that Signor Sandro had been setting forth so eloquently. But he understood that his priest approved the measure. So he said :—

"I am sure, Signor Sandro, that we are very much obliged to you, on poor Giulia's account; and, since *il Signor Curato* thinks well of it, it can't be other than right. I should not have liked the girl to go to service, because it's well known that none of the Vannis ever did go to service," repeated the farmer once again.

"And then, you know, my much esteemed Signor Vanni, I will not attempt to conceal from you, that to a certain degree, I had an eye to other considerations,—to a certain degree, I say,— and hoped in this matter, as I may say, to kill two birds with one stone."

"Which was th' other bird, then?" asked the farmer, bluntly.

"Well, now, I would bet a wager that his reverence the *Curato* has already guessed my thought upon the subject! Is it not so, your reverence?" asked the little man, putting his head on one side, and looking at the priest in

a way that seemed to claim the fellowship of a
kindred high intelligence.

"You have been thinking, Signor Sandro, that
it might be just as well to remove *la* Giulia for
awhile from the companionship of our young
friend Beppo, if we are to hope to bring those
arrangements to bear which I had the honour of
proposing to my friend Vanni. That was your
worship's thought, I take it ; and I agree with
you."

"' *Rem acu tetigisti*,' which means, as your
reverence knows better than I can tell you, that
you have exactly hit the nail on the head !
Dont you see it, Signor Vanni ? "

" I see that I don't mean to allow our Beppo
to have anything to say to Giulia,—not in the
way of marrying ;—it isn't likely."

" Well, then, my dear sir, since we have our
eyes on a young lady, who may perhaps with
better reason pretend to the honour of an alliance
with Signor Beppo, and since youth is sometimes
apt to be blind and self-willed in these matters,
does it not appear to you a judicious measure to
remove the source of danger ? "

" Surely, surely ! And I do hope that, when
she is gone, the lad will come round, and not

break my heart any more!" said the old farmer.

"Ha! the best way to exorcise the charm, is to pack off the charmer, in these cases. Is it not so, your reverence?" laughed the attorney.

"I think, as I have said, that your proposal is a sound and judicious one, Signor Sandro," replied the priest, "both with a view to our young friend Beppo's advantage, and as likely to be exceedingly useful to *la povera* Giulia."

"Then we may consider the matter as settled. I am sure I shall have killed *three* birds with one stone, and rendered a service to my old friend and client *la* Signora Clementina into the bargain. I have no doubt she and *la* Signorina Giulia will get on capitally together!"

"And we are all very much obliged to you, I am sure!" said the old farmer, a little more graciously than he had spoken hitherto. "When do you think that *la* Giulia had better go to her new home?"

"Well! of course I would not say a. word to Signora Dossi till I had consulted you, I am quite sure she will be only too glad to get such a prize as the Signorina Giulia. I must see her, and settle about it. I should suppose it would be a

case of the sooner the better!—perhaps next
Sunday. You would then be at leisure to bring
her into town yourself, Signor Vanni ; and see
my good friend Signora Dossi, which will be
satisfactory to you. Would that suit you ?"

"Yes, I could bring Giulia in on Sunday very
well! Yes, that would suit very well!" replied
the farmer.

"And then you should come and eat a bit
of dinner with me, you know, before returning
home," added Signor Sandro, rubbing his hands
cheerily.

"Well! thankye! You are very good! That
would all suit very well! On condition, however,
that you will come up and dine at Bella Luce
on Lady-day," put in the *contadino* pride.
"Is it a bargain ?"

"With pleasure, my dear sir! There is my
hand upon it. I would ask my friend Beppo to
come with you on Sunday, only—— ; you understand. There would be no use in long leave-
takings, and chattering, and nonsense ; you comprehend me! And it would be better, perhaps,
if he and Lisa were to meet not so immediately,
but after a little while."

These considerations were quite beyond the

reach of Farmer Vanni's mental powers. He said, however, that "certainly that would be best;" and the priest gave the little attorney an intelligent nod, which the latter returned with half a dozen, accompanied by winks to match.

"It is understood, then, my dear Signor Vanni, that, unless you hear anything from me to the contrary, you bring in *la* Signorina Giulia on Sunday. Come direct to my house, and I will go with you to Signora Dossi. You will find her, and *la* Giulia will find her, an excellent, worthy creature—a heart of gold! At what hour can you be in the city?"

"Oh! early: so as to be back at Bella Luce before the Ave Maria!"

"Then I'll tell you! You must be early enough to go to *la* Clementina, before high mass —say before eleven o'clock. We will dine at mid-day, which will give you plenty of time."

"Thank you. That will do very well. Will you come and have a look at the vines?"

Signor Sandro knew the *contadino* nature too well, and was too desirous of standing well with the wealthy farmer to refuse this invitation. So they strolled out together into the field where Vanni had been at work, and to which his two

sons had already returned. The priest, remarking
that he had a few words to say to *la* Signora
Sunta, remained behind ; and he and Signor
Sandro exchanged an adieu with somewhat more
cordiality than they usually adopted towards
each other.

And thus poor Giulia's destiny was settled for
her, as women's destinies mostly are settled, without their knowledge or co-operation in any way ;
—and the old gentlemen made up their minds
that, when the dangerous charmer should have
been removed, the charm would cease to operate
on the refractory Beppo.

CHAPTER VI.

THE ANNOUNCEMENT.

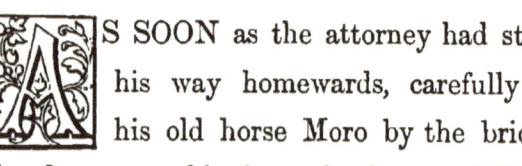S SOON as the attorney had started on his way homewards, carefully leading his old horse Moro by the bridle down the first steep bit from the house of Bella Luce to the bottom of the valley, Farmer Vanni pulled off his jacket and returned to his work of dressing the vines in the home vineyard, without saying a word to any one of the family of the important business that had been determined on. He knew, however, that his wife would hear it all from the priest; but was pretty sure that it would not be mentioned by either of them to Giulia before he should himself communicate the tidings to her. He pondered a little on the question, how and when he should break the news to his son; and eventually de-

termined to say nothing at all to him specially
on the subject;—to mention it to Giulia in his
presence, treating the matter as if it was one
which very little concerned Beppo in any
way.

Don Evandro, when the farmer and the attorney
went out together, passed from the kitchen into
the loggia, where he found *la sposa,* as he thought
he should, quietly plying her distaff and spindle,
seated on the squared trunk of a chestnut-tree,
which had done duty for a bench in the loggia
for more than one generation.

"Signor Sandro came up here to make a proposal which seems to me to have much good
sense in it," said the priest, sitting down by the
side of Dame Assunta, and offering her a pinch of
snuff as he spoke.

"A proposal, your reverence? And what was
that?"

"Why, that this troublesome, headstrong girl,
Giulia, should be sent to service in Fano, to a
place he has found for her. Of course he has
his own object to serve."

"To service! Will Vanni consent to that?
None of the Vannis ever *did* go to service!"

"He has consented. The lawyer made it out

that it was not altogether a regular servant's place ; and in speaking to Vanni, you must not call it so, mind."

"He has consented ?"

"Yes! of course he did! It is a very good thing. What is the use of letting those two go on in the house together ? The only way is to part them! Don't you see ?"

"I don't think she gives him any encouragement !"

"Bah—h !" cried the priest, shrugging his shoulders, and drawing out the expletive into an expression of the most utterly contemptuous unbelief. "She has got eyes in her head! I tell you, the only way is to separate them."

"Well, I am sure, if your reverence thinks so—— But I am afraid he won't forget her a bit the more ! He isn't of the sort that forgets. The Vannis are all terrible holders-on to anything they once lay hold of,—terrible !"

"Forget ! Well, perhaps his remembering may serve our purpose equally well ! Is there no way of falling out with a lover, Signora Vanni, besides forgetting him ? Don't you see ?"

"I don't see what is to serve, unless we can get him to put the girl clean out of his head.

I wish to heaven she had never darkened these doors ; I do with all my heart ! "

" Ah ! It's too late in the day to wish that now ! But, don't you see what will happen ? Look at that girl ! You don't see such a girl every day. Do you think the men won't come round her down in the city, there, like the flies come to the sugar ? And she with her spirit and giddy laughing ways, and eighteen years ! You don't think she is going to mope and pine, and think of nothing but Beppo ! And he need not fancy anything of the kind."

" I am quite sure the hussy will see nobody so well worth thinking of ! " said the mother.

" That's very likely. But she will think of what's under her eyes ! The fellows will come round her ! She can't help herself if she would ! Then, what follows ? Beppo will be jealous—angry —furious ! He will hear all her goings-on. Of course he will ; it will be our own fault if he does not ! And it's odd to me if we can't bring him to the point of marrying the first girl ready to have him ! "

" But *is* Lisa Bartoldi ready to have him ? " asked Signora Anunta.

" That will be Signor Sandro's business to see

to. A girl is always more easy to manage than a boy, in these cases. And such a girl as Lisa Bartoldi! I have seen her. There will be no difficulty with her. Signor Sandro has only got to say that it is what he chooses!"

"You think so!"

"*Altro!* no doubt of it. So you see, *signora mia*, this plan of sending *la* Giulia to the city may serve our turn, even if we don't persuade Signor Beppo to forget all about her," said the priest, looking at her with a smile that was half a sneer.

"I hope it may; and I've no manner of doubt that your reverence knows what is best and wisest," said the farmer's wife, submissively. "Had I better tell Giulia that she is to go?"

"I think not. No doubt Signor Vanni will speak of it this evening. Perhaps you had better leave it to him to mention it."

"Yes, I think I should like that best. Giulia is a good girl, poor thing, and submissive enough, mostly; but now and then she will break out, and then there is no speaking to her. I declare I have shaken in my shoes as I stood up to her, before now, though you would not think it."

The priest smiled a peculiar smile, and took a pinch of snuff.

"It comes like a flash of lightning with her," continued Signora Vanni, busily twirling away at her spindle as she talked, "and it's all over in a minute; and then she runs away and shuts herself into her room. Yes, I should like best that Vanni should tell her himself. Is it fixed when she is to go to Fano?"

"Signor Vanni has promised the attorney to take her himself next Sunday, if he hears nothing from him to the contrary," replied the priest, quietly.

"Next Sunday! And this is Thursday! Mercy upon us! that's very sudden! And her things! The poor girl should be sent decent, you know. She is a Vanni, after all!" remonstrated the *padrona*, no little startled by the abruptness of the proposed measure, though her surprise did not avail to arrest the habitual plying of the spindle.

"The only question is, whether the time between the telling her and the sending her off is not too long, as it is," said the priest. "I should have preferred letting her know nothing about it till Vanni called her to start with him for Fano!"

"But her things!" exclaimed the mistress of the house, whose housewifely notions of propriety were painfully shocked by the idea of having only forty-eight hours allowed her for preparation in that exclusively female department.

"Anything that is not ready can be sent after her. Do you not perceive," continued the spiritual adviser, "that it is by no means desirable that there should be much opportunity for leave-taking and exchanging of promises, and vows, and tears, and all that sort of thing?"

"Oh, dear! I don't think that Giulia would give in to anything of the kind. I don't, indeed, your reverence! Bless your heart, if we had seen anything of that sort, we should have made short work of it before now, you may depend on it! Oh, no! Giulia is a sensible girl, and knows her place; though she does go off into a fit of tantrums now and again. Though I am his mother, I must say that the foolery has all been on Beppo's part. But, there! we know what young men are! It was so in my time! And, though they do talk so much about the world being changed, I suppose it's much as it was, in that matter."

"Well! if you will take my advice, you will

just keep an eye on them, as much as you can,
for these two days, and don't let them be together
a bit more than you can possibly help."

"I'll take care, your reverence!"

"And, look here!" said the priest, as he rose
from his seat on the chestnut log beside her, and
turned to leave the loggia, you can send her up
to the cura to lend Nunziata a helping-hand.
I'll tell *la* Nunziata to detain her all day; and
that will help to keep her out of his way one
day, at all events."

"Yes, your reverence."

"Good afternoon, Signora Vanni."

"Good afternoon, and many thanks, your
reverence."

Breakfast, as a meal, is not known to Italian
peasants, and is not a matter of much moment
to the inhabitants of Italian cities. In the farm-
houses, the usual practice is to eat at mid-day,
and again when the day's work is over in the
evening. And there is very little difference, if
any, between the two meals. *La zuppa* is the
standing dish, generally the most important;
and, in the poorer families, often the only dish
at either meal. There is far less difference,
however, between the more easily circumstanced

and the poorer families of the *contadino* class,
than is the case among our own rural population.
The poorer are less hard pushed than are our own
very poor ; and the richer are more thrifty,—
more niggardly, if the reader please,—and more
given to saving, than our own people when in
easy circumstances. A rich Italian countryman
likes to make a show of his wealth ; but it is
only done on special and rare occasions and
solemnities. The general staple of his life is
fashioned on very much the same plan as that
of his poorer neighbours.

The whole of the feast spread before the unexpected visitor at Bella Luce, the *menu* of
which had been rehearsed by the mistress of
the house with almost as much ostentation as
that which struts in the written *cartes* of more
aristocratic houses, had been, with the excep
tion of the *minestra,* and probably the rashers,
an improvised addition to the family repast.
And at supper-time, the remnant of the *frittata,*
and a fragment of the fowl, furnished an un-
usually luxurious second course after the never-
failing *zuppa* or *minestra ;* the difference between the two being, that the first is made
with bread *sopped* (*inzuppato*) in broth, and

the second always with some form of what is known in England as maccaroni, but which is more commonly called in all parts of Italy, save Naples, *pasta*. The latter is often, especially in the north of Italy, eaten with so large a proportion of the solid material, to so small a quantity of the liquid, as no longer to correspond with our idea of soup at all.

Giulia did not make her appearance again in the kitchen, till she came out from her hiding-place to prepare the evening meal. On any other occasion *la* Signora Vanni would probably have been after her before that time, to see that the spindle was duly twirling, and the ball of yarn on it duly swelling; though, to tell the truth, Giulia was not an idle girl, and generally got through the hank of flax on her distaff in as short a time as *la sposa* herself. But upon the present occasion, the mistress was not anxious for a meeting with Giulia; and the latter attributed the unusual prolongation of the privacy permitted to her to the dish of chat with the priest, which she knew Sunta was enjoying, and which she supposed was being prolonged during the whole afternoon.

When she came into the kitchen to perform

her evening duty, *la sposa* was not there; and Giulia prepared the supper by herself.

The usual hour came; the sun was dipping his red disk behind exactly that bit of the crest of the Apennine, which he always touched every evening at the time when the vines were being pruned, and was flinging a great glowing patch on just that section of the far-off Adriatic, which was visible from the mouth of the Bella Luce valley; and Giulia, having completed her preparations for the evening meal, was standing at the door dreamily looking out at the slowly fading glory, when the farmer and his two sons came strolling slowly up from their light day's work.

Reverie is generally accompanied by a graceful position and arrangement of the body and limbs. It is not advisable to practise reverie with a view to attaining this result, inasmuch as the intention would suffice to prevent the desired effect;—the cause of the fact being simply this, that reverie presupposes an absence of self-consciousness, and, therefore, ministers to grace exactly as an excess of self-consciousness mars it and insures awkwardness and affectation.

Giulia's attitude, as she stood at the kitchen-door, is chargeable with this little *excursus*. It was singularly graceful; and her figure as she stood, so that a slanting ray just caught and lent a glory to her head, while the rest of her person was in shadow, if only it could have been transferred to canvas by some artist, who would have been contented to add nothing to what he saw, would have made the painter's fortune.

She was dressed in that mixture of colours so much affected by the Italian peasantry—red and blue. She had a blue skirt, a scarlet body, and white linen sleeves. The skirt was short enough, and the shoe cut low enough, and the white stocking well drawn enough to show to proper advantage a specially trim ankle and well-formed foot. The scarlet body fitted well enough to set off admirably all the contours of a bust such as is rarely seen in cities—rarely among the over-luxurious rich ; more rarely still among the imperfectly nourished poor. A little frilled collar, scrupulously clean, circled the matchless column of a throat, that, sunburnt as it was, carried the head so exquisitely poised upon it, in a manner, and with a proud expression of unconscious dignity, which would have become a maiden queen. The rare abundance of raven hair was neatly, and, indeed, artistically arranged in masses on the sides and at the back of her head. A long silver bodkin, with a large round head of filagree work, was passed through the knot of it at the back. She was standing with her left shoulder slightly leaning against the door-post; the elbow of her right arm was resting on the palm of her left hand; and her chin, somewhat drooping, was supported by her right hand.

If it be asked whether all the girls in the farm-houses of the Romagna have their collars as scrupulously clean, and their whole costume as neat and attractive as that of Giulia Vanni undoubtedly was, I can only say that I have every reason to believe that the Romagna girls have the peculiarity of always appearing so when they live in the same house with such a young man as Beppo, whom they consider it to be their duty to keep at a distance.

The beauty of Giulia's figure and attitude had not been lost on Beppo, as he approached the house. His eye had eagerly sought the doorway; for it often happened that she stood there a few minutes at that hour to look out on the sunset sea and landscape. But as soon as she saw him—was it *quite* as soon?—she flashed

away like one of those pretty bright lizards of
her country, which may be watched basking on
a stone as long as they are unconscious of the
watcher's presence, but which flash out of sight
with the speed of lightning as soon as they become aware that they are looked at.

Giulia vanished, and did not show herself in
the kitchen till the men and the mistress of the
family had taken their places at the supper-
table.   Then she slipped in and quietly took
her usual place on the bench next the wall, by the
side of the Signora Sunta.   The farmer occupied
one end of the long narrow table, and the two
young men sat on the outer bench, opposite to
their mother and cousin.

The meal proceeded in silence till the soup had
been eaten, and then the farmer said, " There ! a
man can talk better when he has got something
in the inside of him, especially when he has been
in the fields all day ; and I have got something to
tell you.   There is a *benedizione del cielo** for
you, Giulia.   What should you say to going to
live a spell at Fano, to learn—all manner of
things that city-folks know, and that you might
live up here everlasting without ever knowing ?"

* A popular phrase for a great and unexpected benefit:

"Me, Signor Paolo!" said Giulia, looking up in amazement.

"Yes, you!—who else? And, to make it short, it don't much signify what you think of it, for it's all settled. There's a place found for you!"

"A place! Go away from Bella Luce!" gasped Giulia, while the open scarlet bodice began to rise and fall very perceptibly.

Beppo had remained fixed, as if suddenly turned to stone, with his mouth open, one hand with his fork in it raised in air, and the other grasping his knife, held bolt upright on the table, staring at his father, and making but slow progress as yet towards realising the full import of the announcement.

"Yes, a place; and a very good one too!" resumed the farmer.

"Oh! Si'or Paolo! please don't send me away! I'll work harder and spin more! Don't send me to service! I'd far rather live always at Bella Luce!" said poor Giulia, wholly unconscious of the possible construction that might be put on her last words.

"Always live at Bella Luce! Ah! that I'll be sworn you would!" sneered the old man, bitterly and grimly; "but that is just what I don't mean you to do, my girl!"

The blood rushed in an impetuous torrent all over Giulia's brown cheek, and over her forehead and neck. Her ears tingled, her hands burned, and she felt as if she should have choked. It was some relief to her to know that no one of the party save the old man was looking at her. Beppo was still staring in speechless dismay at his father; and Carlo was watching his brother with a malicious smile. The eyes of *la sposa* were fixed upon her plate. With a mighty effort of will, Giulia prevented herself from sobbing or giving any other outward sign of her distress. Presently all the tingling blood flowed back again, and she sat as pale and motionless as a corpse, with her eyes fixed on the table.

"And what do you mean by talking about service?" continued the farmer, angrily. "Who said anything about service? You are not going to service; and you are never to speak of your position as such. None of the Vannis ever did go to service; and you are a Vanni, worse luck! You are never to speak to any one of going to service, do you hear?"

"But, father, everybody will know it! You

can't think to keep it a secret!" said his son Beppo, at last, flattering himself that he had found an unanswerable argument against the measure.

"You hold your tongue, booby!" said his father, roughly, yet with a very different sort of manner from that in which he had spoken to the stranger within his gates. "Believe me, you know nothing about it. What I mean is, that the place Giulia is going to is not the place of a menial servant. Do you hear, Giulia?"

"Yes, Signor Paolo!" said Giulia, now able to speak calmly, in a low, submissive voice.

"And you understand that you are never to speak to any one of being in service?"

"Yes, Si'or Paolo!" repeated Giulia, still keeping her eyes fixed on the table.

"And his reverence quite approves of it; and thinks you ought to be very thankful for your good fortune! Do you hear?"

"Yes, Si'or Paolo!"

"And Signor Sandro, who was good enough to think of you, and to find this fine opportunity, and to ride up here to-day on purpose to bring the offer of it, says that it's a very advantageous thing!"

"Was it Signor Sandro's kindness to think of this scheme?" asked Giulia, looking up at the farmer for a moment.

"Yes, it was! and very kind of him, I take it!" replied the old man.

"Very!" said Giulia, while a very legible sneer curved her lip into a form of beauty that was not habitual to it, and flashed in one brief gleam out of her eyes, before she again dropped them on the table.

"Do you think it necessary, Si'or Paolo," she asked in a hard, constrained sort of tone, after there had been a minute or two of silence, "to send me away from Bella Luce, for—for—your own views, as well as for my advantage?" She knew that the old man would understand her, and that the others, at all events Beppo, would not.

He looked hard at her, as he answered, "Yes, I do think it is necessary."

Giulia set her teeth hard together, and clenched her hands under the table till the nails nearly cut the skin, while a little shiver passed over her, leaving her as rigid, as pale, and as hard-looking as marble. And she said nothing more.

"But you have said nothing about the time, Paolo!" said *la* Signora Sunta, who, with the difficulty about "the things" heavy on her mind, felt that the worse part of the farmer's communication still remained untold.

"The time! why, as his reverence said, and Signor Sandro said too, the sooner the better! You can't be too much in a hurry to make sure of a good thing! I shall be able to go into Fano with her on Sunday; and that will be the best day. It was all settled so with Signor Sandro!"

"It'll be very difficult to get anything ready at all decent by that time! Do you hear, Giulia, my girl! You are to go on Sunday!" repeated *la* Sunta; for Giulia gave no sign of having heard a word more since the last answer the farmer had given to her question.

"Yes, Si'ora Sunta; I hear!"

"Well! how ever we are to get your things ready by that time, I don't know!"

"It won't signify much about the things!" said poor Giulia, making a very narrow escape from letting a sob escape her (and she would rather have knocked her head against the wall than have done so!) as she spoke.

"Nonsense! don't signify! Why, you must go decent, child! You are a Vanni, after all!" remonstrated Signora Sunta.

"Worse luck!" said Giulia, re-echoing the far-mer's previous words.

The old man scowled at her, but said nothing.

"Come upstairs with me, child, and help me to see what there is to be done. And thank God that you *are* a Vanni, and have got decent people to think for you and care for you!"

So Giulia got up and followed the *padrona* out of the kitchen, venturing as she passed to cast one furtive sidelong look at Beppo from under her eyelashes. It was by no means intended to meet any look of his. It was merely a look of observation.

It found him still in a state of collapse from the extremity of his astonishment and dismay.

CHAPTER VII.

MAIDEN MEDITATIONS.

WHEN Giulia at last escaped from *la* Signora Sunta, and the inspection and consideration of " things," and was able to get away to her own little chamber for the night, she felt as if she had been stunned during the last two or three hours, and was only now for the first time able to bring her mind really to bear, with anything that could be called thought, on the communication that had been made to her. She drew the rough bolt which supplied the place of lock and handle on the door of her room through its two rusty staples by its hanging handle, and having thus made sure of privacy, she sat down on the side of her bed to think.

And the thoughts that came were very bitter.

It was not that she was being separated from
Beppo. *Che!* What was Beppo to her? What
could Beppo ever be to her? She had known all
that before; not now for the first time. She knew
very well that he loved her. What was the good
of pretending not to be aware of it? But was
that her fault? And she herself—did she care for
him? What business had anybody to ask that?
What right had anybody to think it? She was
quite sure that Beppo must fancy she hated him.
Had not she always behaved as if she had an
aversion to him? Had she ever sought his love?
Had she not abstained from even raising her eyes
to look on the sacred heir-apparent of the house?
Had she not striven loyally? She knew his position; she knew her own; she knew his father's
hopes and wishes. Had she not been loyal? And
now she was turned out of the house for fear
Beppo should make love to her! And others were
to be consulted! She was to be talked over with
strangers! This smooth-spoken attorney from
Fano—his kindness to her! *Oh bella!* as if she
did not see through his kindness, and understand
it all! Had she tried to stand in the way of his
daughter? Let the whity-brown thing have
Beppo, if she could catch him. She had a cer-

tain amount of doubt about her success in that respect; even though she, the poor cousin, were turned into the streets to secure it!

It was hard to bear; very, very hard! How cautious she had been! how proudly determined never to allow room for a suspicion that she had abused the charity of which she was the object, to the securing of a rich marriage! Cautious!— she had been cruel in her proud humility, yes, cruel to poor Beppo—honest, frank, simple, loving-hearted Beppo. Love her! That he did. At all events, she would never be guilty of the hypocrisy to herself of pretending not to know how truly, deeply, devotedly, untiringly he had loved her! And how proudly cold she had always been to him! How she had denied him every opportunity of being alone with her! How she had affected not to understand his simple, honest love-making, to despise his bluff, awkward compliments; to turn away from the frank, loving glance of his great blue eyes! And all for this! And as these thoughts passed through her mind the hard, proud mood gradually faded out of it, the lip began to quiver, her breath came short, the tears gathered slowly in her eyes; and presently, as a special recollection crossed her mind

of poor Beppo's look, when at his last *ceppo* he
had walked into Fano, and bought a neck ribband
of a colour she had praised, and she had told him
at his return that he had better give it to Nina
Sganci, at Santa Lucia, for that she had changed
her mind, and should never wear that colour
again. A passionate agony of weeping seized her.
Oh ! how she saw before her his look of pain and
disappointment, as he flung the despised gift
behind the kitchen fire ! And she threw herself
down on the pillow, sobbing at the thought as
though her heart would break.

But when the paroxysm of uncontrollable weeping had in some degree subsided, she began to
question herself about her future conduct, especially on the immediate occasion of her departure.
Beppo would endeavour to speak with her;—to
bid her farewell, at least. Was she to take care
that he got no opportunity of doing so ? Was it
likely that he would confine himself to a simple
farewell ? Would not so fair, so plausible an
opportunity, be seized for saying something else
as well ? And how was that something else to be
answered ? Must her answer—her final answer
to him—be of a piece with all her past conduct ?
Had his father deserved of her that it should be

so? Was she bound in honour and in gratitude for the charity, that was now about to be withdrawn from her, to continue to sacrifice his happiness, and—her own? Yes! the hot blush came with the thought, though no human eye was there to see it. It was the sacrifice of her own happiness. Yes! Conscience had spoken the truth! Let it stand. She would affect or attempt to deny it no more. Was she bound to continue this self sacrifice? Had she not done enough? Might she not consider all accounts to be squared between herself and Paolo Vanni? In that case, with how different a heart should she go away from Bella Luce, and face the world! In that case—ah! would not the little attorney's interference turn out to have been a blessing? In that case—at the delicious moment when those dear, honest blue eyes should look once again so wistfully into hers, and she should be able with one glance and half a word to let him know that all the past had been a delusion and a falsehood;— that the cruel duty, which had coerced her every word and look, was a duty no longer! And Beppo would know at last that she was not cold, nor proud, nor capricious, nor insensible. Ah! the happiness of giving this happiness!

But hold a moment! Was it solely duty and gratitude towards Paolo Vanni, and respect for his wishes, that had governed her conduct towards Beppo? Why had she felt at supper time, when he had misunderstood, or affected to misunderstand, her unlucky speech about her wish always to live at Bella Luce,—why had she then felt as if she wished the earth to gape and swallow her up? Surely that was not all because the old farmer seemed to suspect her of ungratefully opposing herself to his will! If he had accused her of any other form of ingratitude, would she have felt the same? No! assuredly she would not. There was some other feeling then at work, to stir her heart so powerfully and painfully?

She honestly then set to work to discover the nature of this other feeling.

Like to live at Bella Luce! She, the poor, portionless, destitute orphan! No doubt!—said old Paolo Vanni. And oh, what agony it had been to hear and see his sneer, as he spoke the words! Would nobody else say and think the same? If she were to suffer dear, honest Beppo to love her, would not the world also sneer, and say, that she liked to live at Bella Luce,—especially as its mistress? And could she endure

that ? Would not men tell each other, that the
worst day's work old Paolo Vanni ever did, was
when he brought the orphan girl home to be
received into his family ? Would it be tolerable
that such things should be said ? Would not the
women say, that she laid herself out for poor
simple Beppo's admiration,—had baited the hook
with smiles, and who knows what else, and
cleverly caught her fish ? Could, oh ! could she
bear that ? And for all the family, and the
friends and relatives to look on her as an unwel-
come intruder, who had pushed her way among
them by——. Oh, it made her turn sick, and a
cold shiver pass over her, to think of the filling
up that would be supplied to that blank !

Like to live at Bella Luce, would she ? I dare
say ! And poor Beppo too ! Lord bless you, *he*
never suspected anything !

No ! no ! no ! she could *not* bear it ! Death
rather, a thousand times rather than such agony !

Bless you, sir, she snared him like a bird in a
springe ! He had no chance with her—there in
the same house with him ! And he so simple and
honest too ! Ah, she was a cunning one ! Love !
don't tell me ! Yes, I dare say, she was in love
with the broad acres of Bella Luce. Ah, it was

a bad day for the Vannis when that sly baggage
came into the house;—and she without a smock
to her back. Why, if it had not been for her
wiles and lures, Beppo might have had old Sandro
Bartoldi's daughter; and what a match that would
have been!

And then the women would smile, and cast
their eyes down, and say that a woman could
always bring a man to her lure—if she chose to
do so! Only it is not every woman, nor many
women, thank Heaven! who would do it.

No! These things should never, never be said
of her. No! Though her heart broke in the
struggle. No! Though she should be obliged
to keep a smiling face to-morrow, while her heart
was dropping tears of blood. Ay, to-morrow! it
would be a hard task that morrow,—and the day
after! A hard and difficult task.

Poor Beppo, too! How he would be pained!
How she must torture him! Avoid all possible
meeting! That was the only way! No good-
byes! No leave-takings! That would never do!
She would not answer for herself, if on the eve of
parting, those honest, loving eyes got a chance
of looking full into hers, while Beppo asked her
if she had no word for him,—if all his many

years' faithful love must go for nothing? How could she trust herself to answer that? No, no! no leave-takings!—no last words!

"Good-bye, Beppo!" with a nod and a saucy smile, while turning on her heel to go.

She acted the scene as the thoughts passed through her mind, and burst afresh into passionate and bitter tears in the midst of it.

Sudden as a flash of lightning the thought dashed through her brain, "Could Beppo have understood these horrid words, at dinner, as his father understood them? Did he, too, think that living at Bella Luce might mean ——" She started to an upright position, and put her hands to her forehead, as if to help her mind to answer this question. And the answer came from the depth of her own heart, with assurance of its truth. No! No such thought would have found entrance into Beppo's heart. He was too good, too frank, too honest,—and—and—and loved her far too well!

And to leave him with the pain in his great loving heart without a word!

But no doubt he would soon console himself! There were plenty who would like to live always at Bella Luce. Was there not Lisa Bartoldi, a

city lady, as fair and dainty as snow, and as rich
as a Jew, ready to give him all the love of her
heart? Oh! no fear of his pining!

And then she told herself that it was a lie—
a wicked lie to say so! She knew that Beppo
would never love Lisa Bartoldi. She knew that
he would not console himself. She knew that
none other than she could console him. She
knew that he could love no other! And yet she
must be mute, and say no word. She must be
hard—hard as marble! cold, indifferent, gay as
ever!

Oh! would to Heaven that these next two
days were over! Would to Heaven that it were
all over!

And then she cried herself to sleep.

The next morning *la padrona* would have
availed herself of the priest's hint, and sent Giulia
to the parsonage to be out of the way, had it
not been that the question of "the things" was
still pressing too heavily on her. So she kept
that resource in reserve for the next day, the
Saturday, before the Sunday fixed for Giulia's
departure; and determined to keep her under her
own eye all that day, assisting in the work of
getting ready. Giulia acquiesced more than wil-

lingly in the commands of Sunta, to this effect.
She was very glad to escape any meeting with
Beppo that morning. As it was, she never went
down-stairs till after the men had gone out to
their work in the field.

The great room over the kitchen was turned
into a laundry for the nonce, for the making
ready of Giulia's modest wardrobe; and there
she and *la sposa* worked together till it was time
to prepare the mid-day meal. That Giulia had
no objection to venture down to do, for she knew
that the men were away in the field. But when
the time for dinner came, she had a strong inclination to say that she was not hungry, and
would continue their work up-stairs while Sunta
went down to dinner. But she was afraid of
letting the old lady suspect that she feared
meeting Beppo. She was afraid of the remarks
that would be made, and the questionings. And
especially she was afraid that the inevitable
meeting, which must come, would be worse and
more significative if it were deferred, and if it
followed so unusual an event as her absence from
the family mid-day meal.

So she made up her mind to go down to
dinner. Only when the sunlight streaming in

under the eaves of the farm-house touched that particular beam, which indicated that it was nearly noon, she said to *la sposa*, " Will you go and take the soup up, Si'ora Sunta, while I finish plaiting this collar? I will come down directly it is done."

But as soon as ever the old farmer's wife was out of the room, Giulia ran to the window, which was over the kitchen-door, and looked out on the path by which the men would come home from the field; and carefully hiding herself behind the great heavy *persiane*, so as to be invisible from below, kept watch for their coming.

No chronometer can be more accurately true to time than the Italian peasant is in knocking-off his work at mid-day! They carry no watches, but they never miss the time! It was not many minutes therefore that Giulia had to watch before the men came towards the house. Yes! there was Beppo, with his pruning-hatchet hanging from his loins behind, and his broad, shallow white hat on the top of his curly brown hair, just as usual!

Was he just as usual? Generally the men would come in talking to each other. There was something to be said about the morning's

work between the father and his eldest son ;
but this morning the old man and Carlo were
walking in advance, and Beppo was lagging
behind. Giulia could not help fancying too that
there was not the usual springy elasticity in his
step. He was looking down on the ground as he
walked, and she could not see his face, therefore,
as he entered the kitchen-door below her post
of observation.

Giulia allowed a few minutes to elapse, to give
them time to seat themselves at the table, and
then slipping quietly down the stairs, she noise-
lessly entered the kitchen, and gliding to her
usual place, sate down without raising her eyes
or speaking. The meal passed in silence. Such
a circumstance was not so strange at the table
of a family of peasants, as it would have been at
any other. The peasantry are less given to talking than the people of the towns, especially at
table, unless indeed on the occasion of some
festival. But that is a totally different thing—
not differing in degree, so to speak, from the
ordinary every-day dinner, but altogether in kind.

No remark, therefore, was elicited from any
one of the party around the family table at
Bella Luce, by the silence which prevailed among

them. Nevertheless, every one of them knew
what the cause of it was. Beppo tried hard to
get an answering look from Giulia, as she sate
opposite to him at the table, but in vain. She
held her eyes obstinately glued to the table. He
tried to get between her and the door, by which
she had to leave the room when they got up from
table ; but she perceived or guessed his purpose,
and was too quick for him, slipping through the
door and bounding up the stair to the upper
room, before he could get clear of the bench on
which he had been sitting.

And so the dinner was got over ! The slow
hours of the afternoon wore away in completing
the work of the morning by the two women up-
stairs in the great room. *La* Sunta tried two
or three times to enter on a little talk about
Giulia's prospects, about Signor Sandro's kindness, about the place Giulia was going to ; but
she found her unwilling to talk. She answered
in half-whispered submissive monosyllables, and
seemed utterly indifferent alike to all the little
information Sunta could give her, and her many
speculations concerning *la* Signora Dossi, and the
duties that she, Giulia, would be expected to perform in her new sphere.

But when *la padrona* ventured on a few observations on the expediency of prudence as to her general conduct amid the dangers and temptations of the great world into which she was about to be launched—on the difficulties apt to arise from the combination of good looks such as hers, with poverty and a dependent position such as hers—and on the necessity of remembering always that she was a Vanni, Giulia's eyes gleamed in a manner which admonished Sunta that there were signs of "tantrums" in the air! She raised herself up from the work over which she was stooping, as she stood at the long table, and flashing through the tears that rose to her eyes, at the mistress, who was on the other side of the table, opposite to her, she said,

"Would to God that I could forget it! Would to God everybody could forget it! Would to God a pestilence might blotch my face, and leave me as ugly as——"

"Lisa Bartoldi" was on her tongue. But a sudden thought of all the revelation there was in such a display of temper dashed through her brain just in time to save her from uttering it. The sudden pull-up brought with it too a change of feeling.

"Not that I am ungrateful, Signora Sunta," she added, in a submissive tone, "for all your kindness to me. I hope you will never think so. I know how much I owe to you!"

"*Va bene! Va bene!*" said the old woman, glad that the threatened storm had dissipated itself after one lightning flash and thunderbolt; "there, let us get on with these sleeves and the collar, and then there will be nothing more to be done but to put a new hem to the petticoat; and everything will be ready."

So they bent in silence over their work again. Sunta, considering that it was perhaps natural that the girl should be a little out of sorts at the change before her, and having been sufficiently admonished by the little outbreak that had taken place, did not torment her further by any attempt at talking. Nothing further was uttered by either of them, except such brief words as the work in hand rendered necessary; and before the Ave Maria, Giulia's little *trousseau* was completed.

And then came the supper, which was an exact repetition of the noontide meal. Again Giulia contrived to slip into her place after the others had taken their seats. And again she baffled Beppo in an attempt to gain one word, or at least one look, from her, by cutting off her retreat as they rose from the table.

And then there was another night of tears and passionate outbursts, succeeded by sad musings, which only confirmed her in the determination she had reached on the previous night, that no other course was open to her than an absolute avoidance of any private interview or last words of any kind with Beppo, and at every cost a continuation, for the few more hours that remained to her at Bella Luce, of the repelling conduct she had hitherto observed towards him.

And then, *da capo!*—tears, followed by the sleep that at eighteen years rarely fails to visit pillows so wetted.

In the morning of the Saturday she was still making something to do about the work that had been finished over night, in order to avoid going down-stairs, till the men should have left the house, when *la padrona* came into the room, and told her that she had promised his reverence the *Curato* that Giulia should go up that morning to the *Cura* to lend *la* Nunziata a hand at some work. Possibly, too, his reverence might wish to say a few words to her, before parting with his parishioner.

Giulia perfectly well understood the meaning of this arrangement, and was not at all disposed to quarrel with it. She was well pleased to spend the day at the *Cura;* and only hoped that his reverence's few words might be as few as possible. So she dallied yet a few minutes in the room over the kitchen, till she saw from the window of it the old farmer and his second son go forth to their work in the vineyard! Could it be that Beppo intended to absent himself from his day's work, and keep guard in the kitchen till she should come down! Surely under the present circumstances he would not venture upon such a step as that! What should she do? *Could* she tell *la padrona* that Beppo was alone in the kitchen, and that she could not pass through it except under her escort? She would jump out of the window rather!

She was not left long, however, in her difficulty. She was still standing at the window, not so carefully concealed as when she had been watching for the men to come home, when Beppo came slowly out of the door. He had only been lingering behind a few minutes in the hope that she would come down! When he had stepped two or three paces from the door, while Giulia was sadly marking his drooping head and dejected mien, he turned and looked up at the window. He evidently saw her, for his head was instantly raised and stretched upwards in an imploring attitude. He dared not raise his hands, for his father and brother were yet within sight of him. Yes! he evidently had seen her; but it could only have been for half an instant. For with a backward bound, as if she had put her foot on red-hot iron, she placed herself out of sight behind the shutter; yet so that she could still see him standing in the same attitude in anxious hope for awhile. Then he turned; his head dropped again on his chest, and he dragged his limbs heavily to his work.

Then Giulia hurried down, and flitting like a frightened thing round to the back of the house from the kitchen door,—for the village of Santa Lucia was a little way up the valley, whereas the vineyard on which the men were at work was to the front of the house, looking down the valley,—set off for the priest's house.

His reverence, the *Curato*, was from home when she reached the *Cura;* but his housekeeper, *la* Nunziata, was evidently prepared to receive her. She had rather dreaded to encounter the preachment which she expected from the priest, and had still more shrunk from all the questioning and gossiping which she anticipated from *la* Nunziata. But she was agreeably disappointed in this respect. *La* Nunziata had evidently received her cue. She just said that she was sorry they were going to lose Giulia from Santa Lucia ;—that it was very good of her to give her one more day's help, as she had so often done, before she went ; and then plunged into all the variety of little household matters, which she had, or had made a necessity for attending to.

The priest came home to his dinner at midday, but went out again, after his *siesta*, without Giulia having seen him. She began to flatter herself that the preachment part of the business would be spared her. The day passed better and more quickly than she had hoped ; the evening came, and she told *la* Nunziata that it was time for her to go home. But the housekeeper said that she must not in any case go without having spoken to his reverence ;—that he would soon be in ;—and that her orders were to keep Giulia till he came.

The preachment then was to be administered.

It was about half an hour after sundown when

Don Evandro returned home,—just about the time they would be finishing supper, and going to their rooms to bed, at Bella Luce. As soon as ever he came in Giulia was called into his little sanctum, evidently for the preachment. She ventured, however, on entering, to say— perhaps with a view of shortening the infliction as much as might be,—that she was afraid they would all be gone to bed at Bella Luce, and would think she was very late.

"Yes! they are all gone to bed by this time, except *la* Signora Sunta. I have just returned from the farm. You need be in no uneasiness about the time. I told *la* Sunta to wait for you a little while, as I had not had time to speak to you during the day."

And then came the expected few words. But to Giulia's great surprise, they were not all of the same sort with *la padrona's* little attempt at preaching. Don Evandro spoke very kindly;— said not a word about any dangers of the town, or anything of the sort;—seemed quite uncon- scious of the existence of any such dangers. On the contrary, he spoke of his hopes that the amusements of the city, which were natural and proper for her age, would make her forget the

regret which it was natural she would feel at
first leaving her home of so many years ;—spoke
of the indulgence of *la* Signora Dossi ;—she was
an old woman now, but had been young herself ;
and would understand that a girl, such as Giulia,
was not to be expected to lead the life of a
woman of sixty. He had no doubt that she
would find friends at Fano. Girls such as Giulia
—(a priest's smile here, half fatherly, half gal-
lant)—rarely failed to find them ! Let her culti-
vate any such—prudently and innocently of
course ; but by no means let her imagine that
it was her duty to shut herself up like a nun.

And therewith the priest kindly dismissed her,
telling her that she would find *la padrona* sitting
up for her ; and that she must make haste to go
to bed, as she was to start before daybreak the
next morning with Signor Paolo.

Giulia understood it all ; and smiled to herself,
somewhat bitterly, as she thought how much
trouble they were all taking to secure the object,
which was her own as much as theirs.

CHAPTER VIII.

THE CYPRESS IN THE PATH.

T WAS a walk of about two miles from the village of Santa Lucia to the farm-house of Bella Luce—a charming walk down the valley by a little path through the fields, which took its way just above the steep part of the declivity. What has already been said with regard to the position of the farm-house was equally true of the path in question. The upper ground above it rose in a gentle slope, but the side of the valley below it was much steeper; not so steep as to become a precipice, for it was all pasture land, but as steep as it could well be compatibly with such a purpose. The land on the upper side was mostly tillage and vineyard. Almost all the way,

after the little village was cleared, was through
fields belonging to Bella Luce.

Giulia exchanged two or three "good nights"
with the cottagers standing at their own open
door, or returning homewards in the immediate
neighbourhood of the village ; but after she had
cleared it, the solitude was as perfect as if she
had had all the world to herself. It was a
lovely moonlight night. She knew every step
of the way, and every tree she passed, as well
as the furniture of her own chamber ; and her
sense of security was as complete, and would
have been so at any hour of the day or night,
as if she had been there. So she walked along,
in no wise hurrying, despite the priest's last
admonition, and not insensible to the beauty of
the scene and the hour, and to the sense of
liberty and freedom arising from the entirety of
the solitude.

It was the last time she thought, probably
enough the last time for ever, that she should
walk that path ! She had loved Bella Luce well.
Though all had not been happiness there, she
was sad to leave it—to leave it most likely never
to return. Who knew what might come of this
new, strange life, so different, so vague, so full

of unknown elements and imperfectly-conceived chances and changes? How anxious she had been for these two days to be over. They were over now. The dreaded danger was past. Yes, they had taken good care not to expose her to that. To make all sure, she was to start before daybreak. They need not have given themselves so much trouble. Beppo must have been in bed an hour or more. Fast asleep at that moment, doubtless. Was he sleeping? Did she honestly in her heart believe that he was tranquilly sleeping, knowing that he had seen her for the last time? No, she would have no affectation. She would be honest with herself,—honest as Beppo was. She knew that he was not sleeping; more likely would not sleep that night.

Poor Beppo! She knew that he was thinking of her that minute, restless in his bed, and counting the hours till she was to start, and go away for ever. Well! It was all over now. She might think as tenderly of him as she would, now. She had fought her fight, and had conquered. Yes. Thank heaven, she had conquered. She was glad—oh! so glad—that it was over. She might own to herself now, how dearly—dearly she had loved him!—loved him most

when most she had seemed to drive him from
her. She marvelled how she had ever found
strength and courage to fight and conquer as
she had done. And if—

She started suddenly, and stopped in her
sauntering walk, bending her ear to listen.
There was a very large old cypress of great age,
which the Bella Luce people called the half-way
tree, because it was just about at an equal
distance from them and the village. It stood
right in the middle of the little path which
swerved on either side to pass round it. The
main, most used, and larger branch of the path
passed on the upper side, where the slope of
the valley was not steep. A smaller and very
narrow passage crept round the huge old trunk
on the other side, where the grassy slope fell
away not more than six or eight inches from
the root of the tree. No doubt, had there been
no boys or goats at Santa Lucia, there would
have been no trace of a path on this side.

It was as she neared this tree that Giulia was
startled by a sound, it seemed to her as of somebody hidden on the other side of the trunk of it.
She paused a moment ; but reflecting in the next,
that probaoly some villager had fallen asleep

there while resting on his way home, and that at all events there could be nothing that she need fear, she continued her walk. When suddenly, as she came within a pace of the spot, and was about to pass on the main part of the path, Beppo stepped out from behind the trunk, and placed himself full in the centre of the broad division of the path.

Giulia, whose instant and sole impulse was to escape, made a dash at the narrow strip of uncertain path that passed' on the other side of the tree, intending to run for it to the farm, and having very little doubt that she could out-run Beppo after his day's work.

But the grass was wet with dew, and moreover slippery with the dried pin-like leaves that fell from the cypress. Her foot slipped, and she would have rolled down the grassy slope, had not Beppo with a sudden bound to that side of the path, caught her with his arm round the waist, and placed her again on the path; but so as to be himself between her and Bella Luce. Having done so, he took his arm from her, as hastily as if the touch of her had given him an electric shock.

The whole thing had been so instantaneous, that no word had till then passed between them. For a moment they stood looking at each other.

"Stand out of the path," said Giulia then, with the tone and attitude and gesture that a Semiramis might have used to a slave rash enough to bar her way.

Beppo moved a hair's-breadth on one side, as if constrained against his will to obey her behest. But it was only a hair's-breadth; he still, in fact, barred the way, not only with his person, but with his hands as he raised them, and said in a piteous voice:

"Giulia! oh, Giulia! will you leave me in this way?"

And Giulia saw in the moonlight that the whole of his great stalwart frame was shaking with the intensity of his emotion as he spoke.

The fight was not, then, fought out yet; the victory not yet won: and if Giulia would win it, it behoved her to fight again, to fight now, and that well!

"What right have you to waylay me in this way?" she said; but her voice now shook, and was that of distress and sorrow, rather than of anger. "What right have you to come here to stop me?" she continued, with great difficulty preventing herself from bursting into tears. "It is not good of you. It is not kind. You must have known that if I had wished to speak to you, I should not have kept out of your way."

"It was your wish, then, to go from Bella Luce without saying one word of adieu,—one word of kindness! Oh, Giulia! Giulia! is it possible? Can it be that you wished and intended this!" and his strong, manly voice seemed nearer to sobbing than even her own, as he spoke.

"Of course I intended it! What did your father intend when he fixed to start before daybreak? What did your mother intend when she sent me up to the *Cura* to-day? What did the priest intend when he kept me there till all at home were in bed, or ought to be? What did they all intend?"

"What do I care what they all intended? I thought only of you, Giulia; and I did think notwithstanding — notwithstanding all, that you would not have refused to speak to me,—to part in kindness this last night. Oh, Giulia! what have I ever done, that you should hate me so?"

And as he said the words he clasped his hands together, and held them out towards her, and

looked at her in a way that made the fight a
very hard fight indeed to poor Giulia.

Nevertheless, she was still fully purposed to
conquer. She made a mighty effort to crush down
the rising tide of sobs, to still the tumultuous
beating of the heart, that terribly threatened to
become convulsive—(and if it had, the battle
would have been as good as lost)—and to assume
the old tone in which she had so often answered
him, and by which she had given him — and
herself—so many a heartache.

"Hate you! What nonsense it is talking in
that way, Beppo! You know as well as I do that
I do not hate you. Why should I? We have
always been very good friends; and should be so
still, if you would not—persist so stupidly in
wanting to be something else."

"Something else? Yes; I do want something
else, and something more. You know what I
want, cousin Giulia."

"Yes; you want, like other big babies, just
what you can't have. So now let me pass, and
make haste home, or *la padrona* will be wonder-
ing what has become of me. I *am* really very
angry with you for coming here to waylay me
in this way. And pray what on earth shall you

say to them at home ? "—(a little cold spasm shot
through Giulia's heart as she said the last word)
—"I suppose, as usual, I shall get the credit of
this piece of foolery."

"None of them know that I am out of the
house, except Carlo. They think I am in bed
and asleep," said Beppo, hanging his head.

"Except Carlo ! As if all the village would
not know it to-morrow ! Carlo, indeed, for a
confidant !"

"I could not help it; I hoped he would go
to sleep, and that I could get out of the window
without his being any the wiser. But he would
not go to sleep."

"And a pretty story he will make to-morrow."

"I think not, Giulia. He wanted to stop my
coming—said he would call up my father ; but I
said a few words to him," continued Beppo, as a
look came over him which Giulia had never seen
on his good-humoured face before ; "and he did
not say any more to prevent my coming ; and
I do not think he will speak of it to anyone."

"It will be very unlike him, then. And what
were the words you said to him, that produced so
mighty an effect, pray ?"

"I told him," said Beppo, with the stern look

that seemed to change all the character of his face,
and speaking with a concentrated sort of calmness
unnatural to him, " I told him that if he stirred
from his bed I would knock his brains out against
the wall ; and that if he ever breathed to any
human soul that I had left the house, I would
shoot him like a polecat."

" Beppo !" cried Giulia, in unfeigned astonishment and dismay, "you terrify me, and make
me really hate you"—(she loved him at that
moment better than she ever loved him before).
"I did not suppose it was in you to think such
wicked, horrid thoughts."

"Giulia, I am desperate ! You make me desperate ; you make me feel as if neither my own
life nor any other man's life were worth a straw.
Giulia, say a word to me, look kindly on me, and
I will be good and kind and gentle to all the
world.   Oh, Giulia, don't leave me in my despair
and misery ! Give me some hope, Giulia ; some
little hope, and it will save me ! "

Certainly the fight was a very, very hard one.
It was almost going against her ; and if Beppo
could only have known how nearly it was going
in his favour, he would have conquered. As it
was, it was wholly impossible to her to keep up

the light and would-be easy tone she had attempted at first.

"Hope, Beppo," she said, sadly; "what hope
can I give you ? Even supposing that I felt for
you all that you would have me feel, what hope
could I give you ? Do you not know that there
can be nothing between your father's son and
the outcast pauper who has lived upon his
charity ?"

" Spare me, spare me, Giulia ! Don't say words
which make me feel towards my father as I would
not feel. He is old ; and when men get old they
think more of money. But I would be patient ;
I would never contradict him, if I only knew that
you loved me."

" But it is not only your father, Beppo. What
would all the family say ? What would the world
say ? Would they not say that the orphan who
was taken in for charity had schemed to entrap the
heir ? Oh ! I could not bear it. You could not
bear it for me if you loved me, Beppo."

" If I loved you ! *If* I loved you ! Giulia,
Giulia, it makes me mad to hear you. And to
talk of what the people may *say*, when it is to me
a question of life and death. Say ; why they
would say that Beppo Vanni's good luck was

greater than he deserved—that there was not a
man in all Romagna who might not envy him.
Only give me the right to do it, only give me a
hope that you may be brought to look on me, and
trust me to drive the malignant sneers of any
who dare sneer down their accursed throats. If
you fear the world, Giulia, only let me stand
between you and the world."

"It cannot be, Beppo," she said, shaking her
head, sadly. "It can never be. Let me go
home."

"And leave me thus! Oh, Giulia, you cannot
be so cruel! Think of my wretchedness when you
are gone."

"And I am going to such happiness," said
Giulia ; and the tears began to flow from her eyes
and betray themselves in her voice.

"Why should you not be happy ? You will
find plenty to love you, and some one among
them you can love," said Beppo, bitterly.

"Their love would be loathsome to me. I'll
have no love," said Giulia, now sobbing beyond
her power to conceal it. "No love—no love—"
she said amid her sobs, while a little nervous
movement of her foot on the grass, and the convulsive wreathing together of her fingers, as she

held them in front of her bosom, showed the
extremity of her agitation ; " no love—" she
repeated,—"save yours," was upon her tongue.
She had all but said it. She felt as if she would
have given worlds to say it ; but she choked it
down, and said instead, " Oh, Beppo, how can you
make me so miserable ? "

"I ! I make you miserable ! " said poor Beppo,
in utter amazement.

" Yes ; you do. You do make me—miserable
—by—by—by talking about other—other men
making love to me. I hate them, all—all, I do ! "

Oh, poor, honest, dull, simple-minded Beppo, he
did not see the truth.

" I thought it was talking about loving you
myself that made you angry," said he, in the
extremity of perplexity.

" I hate that too," pouted Giulia, as she shot at
him a glance from the corner of her eye that had
almost the gleam of a smile in it, struggling out
half-drowned in tears.

" But you said you did not hate me, Giulia,"
remonstrated he.

" No ; I don't hate you, Beppo. But now I
must go home directly."

" And you *do* hate all other men," said Beppo,

pondering deeply, and more to himself than to Giulia.

"Do stand out of the way, Beppo, and let me go home. I must go directly, now this minute. Beppo, do you hear me?" she added, for Beppo appeared to be perfectly absorbed in the attempt to draw a conclusion from the different premises which had been afforded him.

"If you hate all other men, and don't hate me, I am the only man you don't hate," said Beppo, proceeding cautiously to the construction of his syllogism, but with a strictly vigorous induction which would have done honour to an Aristotelian.

"I didn't say that," retorted Giulia, with her sex's instinctive rebellion against a logical necessity. "Come, let me pass. I won't stay talking with you here any longer."

"It's a great thing to know that you don't hate me," said Beppo, still meditatively, but looking into Giulia's face with wistful eyes.

"Well, be content with it, then, and let me go home at once. The priest will tell *la* Si'ora Sunta what time I left the village, and then she will know that I must have stopped somewhere on my way. Let me go."

"Don't you think we ought to shake hands at

parting, Giulia ?" said Beppo, hanging his head,
and timidly stretching out his hand a little
towards her.

"Perhaps we ought—at parting," said Giulia ;
and her hand stole out from her side to meet his,
while she turned her face away as coyly as if the
threatened kiss of palm on palm had been the
sacredest of love's mysteries.

Nor was the mountain nymph's instinct so far
wrong. For as those two hands touched, an electric thrill shot through both frames, that made
their breath come short, making Giulia feel as
though she should faint.

"It could not be wrong, cousin Giulia," continued Beppo, very gently drawing her hand
towards him ; "it could not be wrong, since we
are cousins, and since—you don't hate me, just at
parting to give each other a cousinly kiss." He
advanced his face a little, a very little, towards
hers as he spoke.

She remained perfectly still, leaving her face in
the most wholly open and defenceless position.
But she said very decisively :

"No man shall ever kiss me, Beppo, except one
that I love with all my heart and all my soul."

She seemed to speak determinedly enough ; but

yet, Beppo observed she did not take any steps
whatever for withdrawing her face from the very
dangerous and exposed position in which it was.
Her eyes were fixed on the ground, her head was
bent a little on one side, so that the rich brown
and pink cheek was held up to the full incidence
of the moonbeam; one hand was hanging list-
lessly by her side, the other was still imprisoned
within his.

"But if I am the only man you don't hate,
Giulia!" pleaded Beppo.

She made no answer, but the play of the moonlight on the rounded contour of her cheek showed
that it was turned up just the least in the world
more towards him; and still her eyes were fixed
on the ground, so entirely off guard as to be of no
use whatever in giving her notice of any menacing
movement on his part. The opportunity was
irresistible.

"I think as cousins at parting we ought!" said
Beppo, suddenly catching her round the waist,
and meaning merely to have his share of that
inviting cheek which the moonbeam was kissing.
But somehow or other, from some little movement
which she made to avoid the attack, his lips came
down, not on the cheek, but full on hers. "Ah,

Giulia! if you would be my own!" he whispered, as not till after a second or two she drew away her face from his.

"That can never, never be," she said, with a deep sigh and a wistful look into his face; . . . . "and this," she added, hastily, "must never be again! And now farewell, Beppo! God bless you!"

"Let me walk with you to the house."

"No! we part here. If we never meet again, I shall never, never, never forget the spot!" she said, with a little tremor in her voice. "Let me go! Good night, Beppo!"

And with a sudden movement she stepped past him, and saying again, "Good night! God bless you, Beppo!" she set off running along the path as fast as she could run.

Beppo flung himself down at the foot of the cypress-tree, and remained there for some hours, immersed in attempts at working out the logical problem which had been submitted to him. He did not succeed at all to his satisfaction in obtaining any clear and distinct conclusion; but he nevertheless remained with a very strong conviction that his cousin spoke the truth in saying that she did not hate him.

Giulia arrived at the kitchen-door at Bella Luce

quite out of breath with running. She saw that there was a light within it, and a little tap brought *la sposa*, who, as the priest had said, was patiently waiting for her, to open the door.

" His reverence has kept you late, child. It is time you were in bed!" said the mistress, letting her in.

" He had not time to speak to me all day. It was only just before I came away that he called me into his study," said Giulia.

" And I hope you will be a good girl, and abide by all the good advice he gave you."

" I hope so, Si'ora Sunta."

" And now, child, you must make haste to bed. Vanni will call you in the morning. Good night, and good-bye, and I wish you good luck and happiness."

" Good-bye, Si'ora Sunta !"

The next morning, before the sun had heaved his great disc clear of the Adriatic, Giulia was seated by the side of the farmer in his *calessino*, and Beppo, concealed by a corner of the house, was watching her departure with a full and heavy heart, though surely with a less heavy one than it had been before the meeting under the cypress-tree.

BOOK II.

AT FANO.

CHAPTER I.

LA SIGNORA CLEMENTINA DOSSI.

HE small episcopal and maritime city of Fano is situated on the flat sandy shore of the Adriatic, a little to the north of the equally episcopal and maritime city of Sinigaglia, and a little to the south of the equally episcopal and maritime cities of Pesaro and Rimini. The new railroad running in a direct line from Bologna to Ancona, a distance of about a hundred and twenty-five miles, passes through no less than ten episcopal cities, most of them situated on the coast. Notwithstanding, however, the original profession of St. Peter, and the honoured memory of that profession, which

has always been preserved by the Church, it would
seem as if episcopacy and maritime enterprise did
not go hand in hand together. For these Adriatic
cities, as the episcopal element in them has become more and more preponderating, have become
less and less maritime.

A strong family likeness prevails in this group
of neighbouring cities; but they have also their
special characteristics. Fano is one of the least
unprepossessing among them to a stranger. It is
not so dirty as Pesaro or Rimini, but it is still
more sleepy. There are fewer mendicants in the
streets, but then there are fewer living creatures
altogether. The ecclesiastical establishments of
Fano, comprising a wonderful assortment of con-
vents and monasteries of both sexes, and of all
sorts and colours, would seem to intimate that
their spiritual interests were those uppermost in
the minds of the inhabitants. And certainly the
little town seems to have retired altogether from
any active interest in any other matters.

Cities were placed by their founders on sea
coasts with a view to the various valuable advantages afforded them by the "water privilege," as
the Americans say, of such a location. Yet Fano
has not only wholly declined to avail itself of any

such, but has taken care to make it manifest to the most cursory observation, that she owns no connection, or even acquaintanceship with the ocean, her near neighbour. I take it that the notorious restlessness of the Adriatic was too much at variance with the habits of sleepy tranquillity cultivated by the men of Fano.

The little town is entirely surrounded by a lofty wall, in which one jealously small gate opens towards the coast. But even that does not afford the Fanesi any glimpse of the restless and sleepless monster which is so near them. The look-out from it is bounded at the distance of a few yards by a lofty ridge of sandhills, arid, parched, pale brown mounds, solitary and desolate-looking. And the stranger who, having learnt that the Adriatic was somewhere in the neighbourhood, should surmount these and make his way to the shore, at the distance of perhaps half a furlong from the city gates, would find himself in a solitude as complete as that of any mourner who ever went

ἀκέων παρὰ θῖνα πολυφλοίσβοιο θαλάσσης.

Fano and the Adriatic are forcedly neighbours; but they have agreed to see as little of each other as possible.

It seems absurd to anybody who has ever visited this very episcopal little city, to speak of a dull street in Fano : they are all so wonderfully dull. But still there are degrees. During the morning hours there *are* four or five old women sitting behind little vegetable stalls in the spacious grand piazza. (Fish ? *Che vi pare?* when we are not on speaking terms with the sea ! We eat salt fish brought from—Heaven knows where, and try to fancy ourselves an inland town.) And even during the hour of the sacred siesta, there is a dog or two sleeping, or perhaps even mooning lazily about in that heart and centre of the city. There are a few shops, too, in the streets nearest to this centre, the owners of which will consent to part with an article or two from their small store, if you will put them in a good humour by dawdling and gossiping for half-an-hour first, and not attempt to obtrude commerce upon them too crudely and abruptly. And all this is life.

But there are streets in Fano — aristocratic streets of enormous palaces, where no such symptoms of life are ever met with. These are the dull streets. A stray dog in those streets would howl himself into a decline because of the intensity of the solitude ! Long stretches

of blank windowless wall of enormous height,
shutting in convent gardens; other still loftier
walls, with little windows high up in them,
fitted with troughs in front of them, to prevent
the inmates from distracting their minds by
gazing into the too tempting world with all its
pomps and vanities in the street below; immense palaces, so hugely large as to puzzle all
conjecture at the motive which could have led
to their construction, with handsome heavy stone
mouldings and cornices around the windows, whole
ranges of which may be seen boarded up with
rough planks: these things make up the quiet
and aristocratic streets of Fano.

And it was in one of the most quiet and most
aristocratic of these that the Signora Clementina
Dossi lived.

Not that *la* Clementina Dossi, properly speaking, belonged to the aristocratic classes of society,
though the position she now occupied was so eminently respectable as to entitle her to admittance
among the easy-going aristocracy, which mostly
confined its exclusiveness and its prerogative to
occasions of high state and public solemnities,
and the matrimonial alliances of its sons and
daughters.

Forty years or so before the date of Giulia
Vanni's arrival in Fano, Tina Tratti, as she was
then called, had been well and favourably known
through a tolerably large circuit of the cities of
Italy as an actress of no little talent. She had
been a beauty in her day, specially celebrated for
her sylph-like figure ; and had for several years
of her spring-tide flitted from city to city, the
favourite of garrisons and universities, and the
queen of a whole galaxy of green-rooms.

Tina Tratti, however, amid her flittings and
her flirtings, and her triumphs on and behind
the scenes, had kept a sufficiently shrewd eye
to the main chance, and had been a sufficiently
valuable component part of the successive com-
panies to which she had belonged, to have laid
by a very snug little competence by the time her
spring-tide was over. The period had arrived by
that time, however, when the same shrewd appreciation of the world and its ways, which, amid
all the "bohemianism" of her early days, had
caused one record at least of that pleasant time
—her banker's book—to be such as could be afterwards perused with satisfaction, led her to the
decision that it was time to "regularise" her
position in the world. She did so by marrying

Signor Amadeo Dossi, the well-known *impre-sario*, who was not above ten years her senior, who had also laid by a snug little fortune, and who, in finding a wife, and retiring from work, was well pleased to meet with so charming a person as La Tina, whose good sense led him to think that she would be duly aware of all that ought to accompany "regularising her position," and whose little fortune was a very pleasant and convenient addition to his own.

So they quitted the theatre together, and came to settle at Fano. And Signor Dossi had never had reason to repent the step he had taken. The ex-sylph Tina Tratti had made him a very good wife during the remainder of his days; which had come to a conclusion some fifteen years before the time at which her history touches that to be narrated in these pages.

In taking a husband, the actress had looked to the regularising of her worldly position, as has been said; and had successfully achieved that object. When she became a widow, however, it appeared to her that the time had come for a further regularising process. She now inclined to regularise her spiritual position, as regarded the stage to which the next shifting of the scene

would introduce her. And she set about doing
so with the same practical purpose-like good
sense which had presided over her previous meta-
morphosis. She made selection of a well recom-
mended " director," became a member of one or
two sisterhoods, made certain little changes in
her style of dress, was not niggard in "benefactions," was constant at morning mass in all
weathers, and invited more priests and rather
fewer officers to her house than had been the
case during the lifetime of her husband. With
regard to more intimately personal changes, there
really was not very much to be done. She took
up a copy of the "Confessor's Manual," and ran
over the authorised list of sins, with their weights
and degrees of blackness. And she could find
but one which seemed to stand in her way at
all. *La gola !** *La* Signora Clementina *did* like
a good dinner ; and was specially fond of a bit of
something nice for supper ! But after all ! The
first glance showed that " *la gola*" was in the list
of venial and not in that of mortal sins. And
a consultation upon the subject with her new
" director" showed her that, properly managed,
it was so very, very venial a sin, that really there

* The technical theological term for "gluttony."

were some virtues which seemed more dangerous. There were the ordinances of the Church respecting certain days and certain meats, it is true. But then the Church knew that fasting was not adapted to all constitutions. There were dispensations; and really on the whole very cheap! The Church had no wish to injure anybody's health. It would be a sin to do so! And if, after all was said and done, the tender conscience of so exemplary a member of the flock as *la* Signora Dossi, should still give her the slightest uneasiness—why, there was the confessional!— what for, save for the ease and comfort of tender consciences? Yes! but about repenting? "If one knows that one is looking forward to one's little partridge *à la Milanaise* at night?" suggested *la* Clementina, doubtfully. Then it was that the director was put on his mettle, and showed that he was worth his hire. He plunged at once with the utmost intrepidity into a turbid ocean of metaphysics, splashing about long Latin words that sounded to the patient as if he were exorcising a whole legion of devils; distinguishing; dividing mental acts with a dexterity of scalpel equal to the highest feats of moral surgery; striking the boundary line between fore-

knowledge and intention with masterly precision;
taking human volition in his teeth, and shaking
it to that degree that it was a mere tangle of
rags when he had done with it; and, finally, con-
vincing his much edified though utterly puzzled
hearer, that she might look forward to her partridge *à la Milanaise* as fondly as she pleased,
with the safest possible conscience.

The Signora Clementina Dossi, when she thus
regularised for the second time, was no longer the
sylph-like creature that she had been some twenty-
five or thirty years before. On the contrary, she
had become remarkably stout. And what was
odd was that she seemed now to ·be as fond of
calling attention to this latter peculiarity, as she
had once been proud of her as remarkably slender
figure. She had preserved a girdle which she
had formerly worn, and hung it up in her drawing-
room by the side of one which showed the circumference of her present portly person. The former,
which had girdled the unregularised Tina Tratti,
measured some twenty inches; the latter, showing the extent to which worthy Clementina Dossi
had prospered under her twofold process of regularising, exhibited a length of some sixty. *La*
Dossi was very fond of pointing to these two

records, especially if any slim young girls came into her room. She would make them try on the ex-sylph's girdle, and then say, "That is what I was when I was your age, my dear! but t'other is the girth of me now! The Lord has been graciously pleased to increase me threefold!"

And the opportunities for such experiments and warnings were not rare, for young people liked *la* Dossi. She was goodnature itself. She had still pretty, gentle, dove-like eyes, and the complexion of her large fat face was almost as delicately pink and white and as smooth as it had ever been. She had not a wrinkle in it—as, indeed, it would have been difficult for her skin to find the means of making one, so entirely filled out was it by fat. Her small mouth, too, and still perfect teeth, had suffered but little from the effects of time. But underneath the sweet-tempered looking mouth there was a double chin of the most tremendous proportions.

All the young people liked her; and though, as has been said, the complexion of the society which she was wont to gather around her was in some degree modified after her husband's death, the more mundane element was not altogether excluded. (It had been at her house, for example,

now I think of it, that Lisa Bartoldi had first
met Captain Giacopo Brilli). There was nothing
ascetic about her temper or her devotion. She
had no sort of notion that because she was
virtuous there were to be no more cakes and
ale in the world. She thought, on the contrary,
that youth was the proper period of enjoyment,
and was desirous, to the utmost of her power, to
contribute to enabling them to make the most
of it.

La Signora Clementina Dossi inhabited at the
time of which we are speaking a portion of the
first floor of an enormous palace, the rest of which
was untenanted. The residence was one capable
of surrounding with legions of blue-devils any
tenant capable of harbouring such imps. But
Italians are little troubled with blue devils; and
to la Clementina such devils, unrecognised by her
spiritual advisers, were entirely unknown. She
had for a small rent as many vast lofty rooms as
she chose to occupy. There was no noise in the
street to disturb her daily *siesta*, or mar the comfortable process of her digestion, and the palace
was next door to the church she attended, and to
which her " director" belonged.

La Signora had lost her one servant, who had

married, and she was in want of another. That was the simple statement of the case, and all Signor Sandro's euphemisms about a companion, and a *douceur*, and such like, were all mere bosh, intended to make the proposal acceptable to the farmer's family pride—a sentiment which many an Italian peasant nourishes in as high a degree as any long-descended noble.

Nevertheless, the character and kindly nature of Signora Dossi made much of what he had said as good as true. The distance between employers and their servants is much less in Italy than among ourselves, especially between a mistress and her female servants; and both the position and the temper of Signora Dossi were calculated to make the connection in her case really more like one of companionship than anything else. She did most of her own cooking herself—did it *con amore*, and with as much skill as pleasure. It was, after the religious duties of the morning had been attended to, the great occupation of her day; and Giulia, if she profited in no other way by the engagement the attorney had made for her, was sure to carry away with her from *la* Dossi, whenever she might leave her, a very useful knowledge of the mysteries of the kitchen.

La Dossi had no greater pleasure than teaching the young idea to shoot in this direction—unless, indeed, it were in discussing the results of their united labours ;—a part of the business in which she very commonly invited the partner of her toils to share, the more especially as she loved to discuss also at the same time all the *rationale* of the process of preparation.

Such was the mistress, and such the house, to which Giulia was coming, by the recommendation of Signora Dossi's old friend, Signor Sandro Bartoldi.

CHAPTER II.

THE PALAZZO BOLLANDINI.

ARMER VANNI, when he arrived with Giulia at the attorney's house in Fano, did not seem much inclined to accompany her to that of her new mistress. He did not see that he could do any good, he said. The fact was partly that he was shy, as the peasantry always are with respect to the people of the city—even those of a social rank corresponding to their own —although they are at the same time most thoroughly convinced that they (the countrymen) are the superiors in every really good quality, and partly that he did not care to see how far Signor Sandro's representations as to the exceptionally dignified character of the situation were strictly in accordance with the fact. He had a certain amount of doubt upon the subject, and preferred to remain in such a state of ignorance upon it as should justify him in boasting now and hereafter on all fitting occasions that no Vanni had ever been in service.

So he and Signor Sandro, and his daughter Lisa, and Giulia, dined together at the attorney's house ; the farmer started on his way back to Bella Luce, and then Signor Sandro took Giulia with him to her new home. He had never ceased during dinner time eulogising Signora Dossi, and speaking in the most glowing terms of Giulia's good fortune in having obtained a position in every way so desirable.

Giulia, however, drew more consolation from a few minutes' conversation which she had found an opportunity for with the gentle Lisa. Of course Lisa was in the first instance an object of no little interest to her. She was perfectly well aware of the wishes and hopes of her father and of Beppo's father with regard to them both. She saw her now for the first time ; and every daughter of Eve will perfectly well understand the quick, sharp glance with which Giulia scanned, measured, surveyed, and reckoned her up. Giulia was not strongly impressed with any high idea of her own personal perfections. The village lads had smiled at her. But Italian peasants do not much pay compliments, except by falling in love with the object that appears to them to merit them. She knew that Beppo had paid her this compliment, but then that might be because they were so much thrown into the way of each other. Nevertheless, her survey of poor pale little Lisa was satisfactory to her. It seemed to her quite as conceivable that a man should fall desperately in love with a little white mouse as with Lisa Bartoldi.

Lisa looked also at Giulia with no little curiosity. The feeling was a different one on her side. She had heard much, as we know, from Beppo about her, and she had every reason to wish that he might be constant to his passion for her. As far as that went, the result of her inspection was satisfactory also. But it was not in the nature of womankind that it should be wholly so. Poor Lisa felt too unmistakeably the total eclipse into which this magnificent Diana of the mountains— magnificent in stature, in colour, in development, in vigour—threw her faded and modest attractions. And then Brilli would see her—of course he would in the house of *la* Dossi ; who could tell with what result ? Heaven grant, at least, that Giulia might be sternly faithful to Beppo. Faithful to him ! But Beppo had declared that Giulia cared nothing for him. She understood very well what his father's purpose had been in bringing this superb creature away from Bella Luce. Alas ! might it not turn out that his object might be served by it in yet another manner, if she should appear as lovely in Giacopo Brilli's eyes as she did in hers ?

Nevertheless, the two girls made friends; for Lisa's nature was a gentle one, and Giulia was in a frame of mind in which any proffered kindness was very acceptable to her. They made friends; and Giulia was in a great degree reassured as to the lot that was awaiting her, by Lisa's account of Signora Dossi and her household. She fully confirmed all that her father had said about *la* Clementina's kindness and indulgence. She explained to her her new mistress's mode of life ; told her the leading facts of her former history, and seemed to consider her on the whole as rather a butt for fun and quizzing, though the best and kindest old soul in the world.

"You'll have to try her girdle on, Signorina Giulia, before you have been in her house half-an-hour. You won't be able to put it on. I can; but then I am such a mite compared to you !"

"Put her girdle on!" said Giulia, in great amazement; "what on earth do you mean?"

"Oh! not the girdle she wears now. That would be a very different thing. You will see. It is a girdle she keeps, that she wore once when she was a favourite on the stage. She had a very beautiful figure, it seems,—very slender; and this girdle shows what she was then. She always makes all the girls try it on. Very few can wear it; I can," repeated poor Lisa for the second time; "but then I am such a little bit of a thing! Though I don't think *la* Dossi can ever have been much taller than me. They used to call her the 'Sylph.' And you'll see what she is now. So!" said Lisa, stretching her arms to their full extent. "And she keeps a girdle, such as she wears now, by the side of the other, to show the difference. Oh, she is such a queer old creature! but as good as gold!"

"Is she a little—?" and Giulia tapped her forehead with her fore-finger significantly.

"Oh, dear, no!" answered Lisa, laughing; "only funny. I know," she added, mysteriously, and in a lower voice, "why it is that my father and Signor Vanni have settled for you to go and live there. Don't you know?"

Giulia was for a moment inclined to be angry at

this unceremonious allusion to matters that to her
were sacred, and wrapped in the secresy of her
inmost heart. But a moment's reflection showed
her both the uselessness and the injustice of being
offended at poor little Lisa's friendly-intended
confidences.

"Yes, Signorina Lisa," she said, sadly, "I know
what I am sent away from Bella Luce for."

"But you don't mind it much, do you? I don't
think I should, if I were you. And you know, I
suppose, why my father wanted it?"

"I suppose so," said Giulia, while a feeling of
startled surprise at the suddenness and unreserve
of her new acquaintance's mode of treating subjects which she only approached shyly and timor-
ously, even in her communings with her own
heart, mingled with her sadness.

"To make a match of it between me and Beppo,
you know. But that will never be! Don't you be
afraid of that! Beppo is for you, and for nobody
else. He and I quite understand one another!"

"But—but, excuse me, Signorina Lisa," stam-
mered Giulia, almost speechless from the extremity of her astonishment; "may I ask if you
understood from Beppo that—that—I had ever
accepted his addresses?"

"He, he, he!" giggled Lisa. "No. He said
that you would have nothing to say to him. Poor
Beppo!—he, he, he! But, between ourselves, we
know what that means. Surely you have played
the cruel long enough, Signorina Giulia! And
poor Beppo absolutely adores you! He is desperate; he is indeed. And, hark! in your ear,"
dropping her voice to a whisper as she spoke,
"you may see him as often as you like at *la*
Dossi's house. Lord bless you! she is not the one
to keep young people asunder. It is there that
I see—somebody!"

"But suppose I don't want to see—anybody?"
returned Giulia, half sadly and half satirically.

"Oh! come now, Signorina Giulia, let us be
friends! I am sure I wish to. And we can help
one another," said Lisa, in a voice of remonstrance.

"I am very much obliged to you, Signorina
Lisa, for wishing to be friends with me. It is
very kind of you. If I can be of any use to you,
I shall be very happy;—you have only to command me! But—but—but I was quite in earnest
in—in—what I said about myself."

The two girls found great difficulty in understanding each other, in consequence of the vast
distance from each other at which they were

placed, not so much by the intrinsic and original difference in their two natures, as by that of their social position, and the mental training derived thence. The contrasted manner in which they felt and spoke on the great subject, which is more important and interesting than any other that can occupy a young girl's mind at their time of life, was exhibiting the different tendencies of the town and country nature. It is true that Giulia's was the deeper, richer and more earnest nature; but that was only in the second place the cause of the notable difference between them. It is the denizen of the town who runs out in fluent, abundant and ready talk. The peasant nature is more reserved, more inarticulate. Less accustomed to constant contact and companionship with others, the *contadino*, and, perhaps, in a still greater degree, the *contadina*, is unready with the tongue, reserved in temper, shy, modest in thought as well as in word, unable to get readily spoken even that which she would desire to speak. It is the town girl who pins her heart upon her sleeve, makes gossip matter of the most delicate secrets, and is ready at a moment's notice to discuss them with any street corner or doorstep female friend.

To Giulia, Lisa's mode of speaking was shocking and painful, as well as extraordinary. She could not understand her. The manner in which she plunged into the sacred places — the innermost holy of holies of Giulia's guarded heart, seemed to her an impertinence; and the way in which she dealt with her own secrets almost an indecency. She was at a loss whether to think her worthless or half-witted.

"How do you mean in earnest about what you said of yourself? What *did* you say?" replied Lisa, quite unconscious of the slightest indiscretion.

"I said that I had no particular wish to—to—to see—a—anybody at the house of *la* Signora Dossi," returned Giulia, casting down her eyes.

"Oh, don't talk in that way! There's nobody to hear but ourselves. You don't really mean that you don't care for poor Beppo. I can hardly believe that. I should be very sorry. And even if you did not, it would be reason the more why you should wish to see somebody else;" said Lisa, reflectively. "You are not—?" she said suddenly, completing her phrase by pantomimically taking an invisible rosary from the side of her dress, where it would have hung from her girdle, if she had worn one, and moving her fingers and lips as if she were going through the exercise of "telling her beads."

"Oh, no!" said Giulia, laughing in spite of herself; "not that at all."

It was the only conceivable theory on which Lisa could explain the case of a girl, who neither had a lover, nor yet was anxious to take the ordinary means towards having one. There was, however, one other means of explaining Giulia's conduct ;—it might be fear, and over-caution.

"Well, then," she returned, "we ought to understand each other. You don't suppose that I should say a word to my father! And what's more, let me whisper in your ear, *la* Dossi won't say a word either. She never tells tales,—had too many secrets of her own to keep once upon a time, I suppose. And she's too good a creature. Lord bless you! Papa thinks she tells him every-thing. So she does, about her money and pro-perty, and such things. But—not matters which don't concern him. Tell me, Giulia dear," she added, sliding coaxingly up to her, putting her arm round her waist, and looking up with a roguish smile into her face, "you do care for Beppo, don't you ?"

"But what does it signify, Signorina Lisa, whether I care for him or not?" said poor Giulia, thus forced against her will into a half-confidence; "you know, even if I did, and he loved me ever so well, there could never be anything between us."

"What! because of the old ones? Bah!—whish —sh—sh!" said Lisa, prolonging her hissing expletive, and vibrating the fingers of one extended hand, in a manner expressing to Italian perceptions the most intense derision and contempt. "Lord bless you!—now-a-days they can't shut us up in prisons—no—nor make nuns of us either," continued the well-instructed city-maiden; "you have nothing to do but stick to it."

Giulia felt an irresistible repugnance to attempting to make Lisa understand what were the feelings that really did place, to her mind, an insuperable bar between her and Beppo. It would have been better for her peace of mind, perhaps, if she had done so; for the light worldly wisdom and town-bred ridicule with which Lisa would have treated her scruples, might have to a certain degree been a useful corrective of Giulia's highminded but exaggerated pride. She felt it impossible for her, however, to do so. She turned the conversation,

therefore, by reverting to the very natural subject of the life which awaited herwith Signora
Dossi.

"She does not keep any other servant, does
she ?" asked Giulia.

"No, only one; but you won't find that you
have any very hard work to do. I should think
you would find it best not to have any one else
in the house to interfere with you."

"But, you say, she has people at her house ?"

"Oh, yes, very often!—not regular parties,
you know. But there are always people running
in and out. *La* Dossi likes it. I think the poor
old soul would *annoiare* herself to death if she
had not people about the house. She can't go
about herself much, you know."

" Why not ?" asked Giulia.

"Why not! Wait till you see, and then you
will know why not. Lord bless you! it's as much
as she can do to walk to the church next door
every day.

" Is she very religious ? " asked Giulia.

" Yes, very—in a quiet way. But she don't
bother other people with it. She thinks it will
come to their turn soon enough."

"But with so many people about the house,

and one servant to do everything, how shall I ever be able to get through ?"

"Oh! you will do very well. She is not like a *gran Signora dell' alto ceto*,* *la* Dossi. She does much of the work herself. She lives half in the kitchen; and you'll live half in the drawing-room. She would not have any common servant girl, look you! So that was how *babbo* came to think of you, you see."

To a certain extent, then, what the lawyer had said about the exceptional nature of the position he was proposing to "a Vanni" was founded in truth.

And then Signor Sandro himself came in from seeing his guest off on his return to Bella Luce; and announced that he was ready to accompany *la* Signorina Giulia to the house of his friend *la* Signora Dossi, and that it was time to be going.

So Giulia and the attorney set off together, Lisa having promised to see her again before long in her new home, and proceeded to the house of *la* Dossi, while Signor Sandro administered a lecture on the manner in which she was to behave towards her mistress, and on her own good fortune in being received into such a house.

* A grandee—great lady of the highest class.

It cannot be expected that our poor mountain nymph, fresh from the Apennine, should enter her new abode without much misgiving. Giulia felt not a little at the unexpected magnificence of the palace at which Signor Sandro stopped.

"Does *la* Signora Dossi live here?" she asked, with considerable awe.

"Yes; here we are! This is the Palazzo Bollandini. The Marchese lives at Rome. *La* Dossi lives on the first floor. There are very few other tenants in the house."

So saying, he led the way up the enormous staircase; and Giulia was more astonished than ever at the magnificence of her mistress's lodging. It was a huge wide staircase, built of yellow Travertina stone, with the steps so easy and shallow that it would have been no difficult feat to ride up it on horseback. The immense panelled walnut-wood folding doors, with chased gilt bronze handles in the middle of each of them, were on a scale of magnificence to match, and Giulia opened her simple eyes wider and wider as these splendours revealed themselves to her.

A small bit of greasy twine, passed through a gimlet-hole in one of these grand doors, by way of a bell-pull, however, struck the first note of the descending scale, which connected the ancestral magnificence of the Bollandini of former generations with the habits and style of modern life at Fano. Signor Sandro and his companion had to wait a long time before the application of the former to the bit of twine—performed, as Italians invariably do, with a whole succession of pulls, as if he were intent on ringing a peal—produced any result.

Signor Sandro was neither surprised nor impatient. He knew that there was probably no one inside, save *la* Clementina herself,—that she travelled slowly, and that she had a long way to travel.

At last, however, the door was opened; and wide as its aperture was, it disclosed a portion only of the still ampler person of the lady of the mansion. There stood *la* Signora Dossi, the ex-sylph, firmly planted on both feet, so as to assign to each of them its fair share of the work of supporting her person, in the attitude generally adopted by persons of her inches—of circumference. There she stood, rather out of breath, but beaming with good-nature and good-humour.

"Signora Clementina," said the little attorney, bowing still outside the door, for it did not seem

to occur to the ex-sylph that the door-way was
still as effectually closed by her own person as if
she had not opened it, "here is the young person
of whom I spoke to you. She came from Bella
Luce this morning; and so I brought her off to
you myself at once."

"Come in! come in! Signor Sandro; and bring
in your young friend, who is to be my friend
too!" said *la* Dossi, in a small piping voice that
contrasted ludicrously with her appearance, turning round as she spoke by means of three separate
steps, and then waddling back into the vast hall
into which the magnificent doors opened.

It was a really grand apartment, loftier than
the rest of the suite of rooms that opened off it,
of great size and admirable proportions, with a
carved coffered ceiling showing remains of gild-
ing, and a half-obliterated painting of gods and
goddesses in the centre. It was lighted by three
large windows looking on to the street, and paved
with square slabs of the same yellow Travertina
stone of which the staircase was built. On the
wall opposite to the entrance there hung an
enormous escutcheon, on which the Bollandini
arms were emblazoned; in one far corner of the
huge hall there stood an old sedan-chair, with the

scroll ornaments about the top, and the carved mouldings around its panels, which showed it to be the production of the last century; and there were four high-backed, square-built, leathern arm-chairs, with plain flat wooden arms, and orna-ments of gilt carving surmounted by coronets on either side of the high straight backs, which as clearly belonged to a yet earlier period. These were placed, two against the opposite wall under the huge escutcheon, and two against the wall in which the door of entrance was, on the left-hand of it. For the door was nearly in the corner, near the street, with the three windows to the right of one coming in. There was another door to match in the other corner on the same side; but that was only a mock door, for uniformity's sake. There were other two similar doors on the opposite side,—that, namely, on which the escutcheon hung; but these led to parts of the palace not in the occupation of Signora Dossi, and were locked up. In the middle of the fourth side, opposite to the windows, was another similar door, which led to the apartment inhabited by the ex-sylph.

And the huge escutcheon, which belonged to the sixteenth century, and the eighteenth century sedan-chair, and the four seventeenth century arm-chairs, were the only bits of furniture of any kind in the room.

Nevertheless it was there that *la* Dossi chose to receive her visitors; for she waddled no further than to the nearest of the arm-chairs in question, and there sat down, leaving her guest to occupy the one opposite to her, some forty feet distant, or to remain standing in front of her, at his pleasure. He selected the latter alternative.

"So this is *la* Giulia! Per Dio! what a creature! God forgive me for swearing! *Ave Maria, gratiâ plena, Dominus taycoo—o—m!*" (The compensatory formula was uttered with the utmost rapidity—all except the last word, which was prolonged in a sort of penitential whine. *La* Dossi was repentant for having been surprised into swearing; but she had a feeling that the good deed she had performed as *per contra*, left on the whole a balance in her favour on the transaction.) "Why this is a Juno, not a parlour-maid, let alone kitchen! My dear, I shall be afraid of you! I shall have to wash all the dishes myself! How she would bring the house down as Semiramide! You should be on the stage, my dear; you should indeed!"

"I trust you will find *la* Giulia quite as well fitted for mere every-day work, my dear madam. I have no doubt that you will soon get used to one another. Giulia, my good girl, you will find *la* Signora Dossi a kind and considerate mistress. Make her your friend, and you will find her a valuable one. You must remember, Signora, that Giulia has lived all her life in the country; and you will have to teach her many things. But you will make allowances; and I am sure that you will find her anxious to please. And now I must run away, for I have people from the country to see me about this troublesome con-scription business at four. All the country is going mad about it, it seems to me; and the people are thinking of nothing but exemptions and substitutes. Good-bye, Signora. Good-bye, Giulia."

"Shut the door after him, Giulia. There; now we can talk, and make acquaintance. How fond the men are of preaching! They are all alike in that. Have not you found them so, eh? Ah! but it is not preaching they give *you*, I'll be bound. That will come by-and-by. Did you leave many broken hearts up at Bella Luce when you came away, eh?"

"Signora!—"

"Did you, now? Half the village, I should think. You are monstrously handsome, Giulia! But I suppose you don't want an old woman to tell you that. There's plenty of a different sort to whisper that in your ear. And small blame to them. And what about cousin Beppo?"

"Signora!" exclaimed Giulia, in a voice made up of two parts indignation to four parts of supplication, and twenty parts of astonishment.

"Well! and ought not I to know all about it? Am not I to be your mistress, and your protector, and counsellor and friend? Hey! do you think I have not heard all about Beppo and you? Do you think I don't know what old Sandro has put you here for? But don't you be afraid. And don't stand there looking as if you were struck speechless. Did not Lisa tell you I knew it all?"

"Lisa said that you were very kind," faltered Giulia.

"Well then, don't you be afraid of me. Why, I've been in love, girl, before you were ever born or thought of. And Tina Dossi is not the one to put a spoke in a true lover's wheel. Never was, and never will be, per——*Ave Maria, gratiâ*

plena, Dominus taycoo—oo—oo—m!"——(La
Dossi, it will be observed, conscientiously and
honourably paid the fine for the intention, even
though the sin was not consummated. But she
put down a proportionably large balance on the
creditor side of the account.) "Now come along
in and see what there is for dinner. Give me
a hand to help me up. Pull away!—that's it,"
said *la* Dossi, slowly rising to her feet, in obedience to a vigorous pull of Giulia's stalwart
arm.

"Well done! You're a capital one at that,
any way. You would not think, Giulia, that I
was once as active and lissome and slenderer than
you! Yes—a good bit slenderer. But then I
was smaller altogether. They used to call me
the Sylph. I look like it, don't I?"

And so chattering, she waddled across the wide
stone floor of the hall to the door in the middle of
the further wall, and led Giulia into the inner
rooms of her habitation. From the hall they
passed through a very small ante-room, very imperfectly lighted only by a borrowed light, where
there were two other doors, one fronting the
great hall, leading into a sitting-room, and one
on the left hand, leading into a snug little room,

once a store-room for linen, but fitted up as a
kitchen for *la* Dossi's special convenience.

"There's my sitting-room," she said, throwing
open the door of it, and showing a tolerably well-
furnished but rather bare-looking room, totally
devoid of any sign of any sort of occupation or
employment; but garnished with sundry prints
of the ex-sylph, representing her in the various
characters and costumes which had made her
fame and fortune in the days of her sylph-hood;
among which, suspended on the wall in a place
of honour, Giulia's quick eye caught sight of the
two contrasted belts hanging side by side, like
the geographical representations of the shortest
and longest rivers in the world; "and there,"
she continued, pointing to a door at one side of
the further wall, "is my bed-room; and there,"
indicating a similar door on the other side of the
same wall, "is yours. There we are, cheek by
jowl, my dear. So you are in safe keeping, you
see. Only the worst is," and she winked at
Giulia, who thereupon coloured up, though she
could not have told why,—"the worst of it is,
that I sleep like a stone two hours every day,
from two to four, let alone all night, and should
not hear if there were a dozen men in the great

hall out there. But you are a good girl, and would not do anything wrong, I know. And this is the kitchen," she continued, in a tone which seemed to indicate that she considered that to be by far the most important part of her habitation; "I generally eat here, unless I have anybody particular with me. It is very comfortable: and the things are hotter, you know. My hour is one o'clock every day, except Sundays. On Sunday I dine at three; so that the girl may always go to mass with me, and have time to make the soup afterwards. And then we have a mouthful of supper at eight. I do like a bit of supper. *Ave Maria, gratiâ plena, Dominus taycoo—oo—oo—m!*" (The extra *oo—oo* showed that this was the weak point in *la* Signora Dossi's conscience.) "And now come, and let us look after the dinner. I would not ask Don Cirillo to come in and have a bit to-day, because I had no maid to help me. I suppose you don't know much about cooking yet?"

Giulia rehearsed her small list of capabilities in this department, but *la* Dossi shook her head, saying, "Well, you will soon learn. Where there is a will there is a way. And it is a pleasure to teach a willing scholar. Now look here——"

So Giulia received there and then her first lesson in city cookery ; and was thus installed into her new mode of life.

And then the mistress and the maid proceeded together to demolish the work of their own hands, amid the critical remarks and dissertations of the elder lady, who sat the while in a huge armchair provided specially *ad hoc*, while the younger, besides eating her own dinner, did the locomotive part of the business of the table.

And before the meal was over Giulia felt quite at home, and intimate with her mistress, and *la* Dossi had coaxed out of her the entire truth as to all her feelings and perplexities in the matter of cousin Beppo.

CHAPTER III.

THE GREAT FEAR.

IGNOR SANDRO BARTOLDI, after leaving Giulia at the Palazzo Bollandini, had returned home to see people from the country about the conscription, he said. The whole country, he declared, seemed to be going out of its senses about it, and everybody, especially the country-people, were wanting information on the subject, the communal authorities respecting the duties which the law required of them, and the young men and their families respecting all the possible grounds of exemption, and the chances and cost of finding substitutes. Subsequently the government took this matter of finding substitutes into its own hands, naming a fixed sum at which the conscript might buy himself off. But at the time in question sub-

stitutes could only be had by private arrangement and bargain, and the trade of procuring
them gave rise to a great many frauds and
abuses.

This dreaded measure had been threatened and
looked forward to with the utmost aversion ; had
been discussed and grumbled over for many
months past ; and now at last it was come. The
law had been duly passed ; proclamation throughout the country had been made, and all the
requisite notices served on the authorities of the
different communes. The mode of carrying out
the measure was as follows :—

The number of men which the province is
required to furnish, in due proportion to its
population, having been fixed, and this amount
having been notified to the authorities of the
provincial capital, the mayor and syndics of the
different communes received orders to return a
full and complete list of all the male population
of their jurisdictions within the legal age. The
lists are to include *all*, without reference to any
claims for exemption. These are afterwards preferred, examined, and allowed, if clearly good, by
the authorities of the provincial capital. No
exemptions, however, on the ground of physical

unfitness are admitted on this first scrutiny, except such as are absolutely notorious, palpable, and unmistakeable ; as, for instance, in the case of a hunchback, or a man with one leg.

When the communal lists have been thus sent in,—and of course the interest of all concerned, and the mutual jealousies of those liable to be drawn, are a guarantee for their completeness,—a day is appointed for the drawing, in the presence of the magistrates, with every provision to ensure fairness, and with all publicity, in the capital of the province. But, as the whole mass of the population (within the prescribed ages) has been submitted to this drawing, and as it is certain that a very considerable proportion of those drawn will be rejected as unfit for military service, this ceremony is by no means decisive of the lot of many of those who are anxiously awaiting the award of their destiny. Thus, if five hundred men are required, he who has drawn No. 501 is, if he be medically unexceptionable, as sure of having to serve as if he had drawn No. 1.

It will easily be understood, therefore, how sharp and anxious an interest is prolonged during the time that elapses between the drawing and the medical visit ; what inquiries, what speculations, what anxious investigations into the previous health of this or that individual, what hunting-up of evidence, what canvassing of medical men.

The proportion of men rejected is considerable in every province of Italy; but it is much larger in some than in others; larger also, as might be expected, in the towns than in the rural districts. Romagna is not one of the provinces in which the rejection is heaviest. But there is another circumstance which may diminish the number of those who have drawn bad numbers,—i. e., numbers within that of the quota of men required, and which may then affect the fate of those who come next on the roll—desertion! That is the time for desertion; that anxious fortnight or so, between the drawing and the inspection. And of course it is the able-bodied men who desert. And this source of failure cannot be calculated on like that arising from medical objections. And in this respect, also, there is a considerable difference between one province and another. And if the rich and healthy Romagnole hills and plains gave a light rate of medical rejections, the desertion rate was specially heavy there, for the reasons which were assigned in the first part of this story.

And the whole interest attaching to that terrible day of the inspection and final making up of the roll, immediately after which the conscripts have to join the depôts, is not confined to the simple ascertaining that this or that man is clearly unfit for military duty, as perhaps ought to be the case. Another element enters to increase the incertitude and complicate the interest.

The medical commission which examines the proposed conscripts, is composed of the medical officers attached to the military administration, and the medical men employed by the respective communes. Now these two component parts of the medical board are swayed by diametrically opposed objects and interests. The object of the colonel or other officer, who is always present, and of *his* medical men, is to obtain the flower and pick of the whole population. He wants, not only men capable of serving, but the finest and best men. Hence the object of him and his medical supporters is to reject on the smallest possible grounds. The desire of the communal authorities on the other hand, of *their* medical men, and of the population generally, is to protect those who have drawn the better or higher numbers, to limit the suffering and the discontent within as narrow a circle as may be, and not to extend them to those who have had reasonable ground to think that they had escaped. Hence arise sharp conflicts between the two authorities, ending of course very variously, according to the weight, or courage, or energy, or skill of the contending parties. And thus another element of great uncertainty is imported into the lottery.

And now the day had been fixed for the drawing up of the communal lists. Little else was talked about in the country districts, and even in the cities the conscription became the leading topic of interest to all men, and certainly not less so to all women.

At Bella Luce the anxiety was certainly as keenly felt as in any homestead of all the district. There were two sons there, but the conscription could not take them both. The monster, ruthless as it was, had some bowels of compassion. It did not deprive parents of an only son! Carlo Vanni therefore was safe! His name would be returned in the communal list, but merely for the formal fulfilment of the law. His claim to exemption would be immediately allowed as a matter of course. But Beppo was of course liable. There was no chance of any objection being made to him. On the contrary, if his number should be at all within reach, it was very certain that the military officers would make every effort to lay their hands on the finest young fellow in all the country side.

But of course it was supposed in the world of Santa Lucia that Beppo Vanni would never have to serve. What! the son of old Paolo Vanni of Bella Luce : Why he could buy a dozen substitutes if needed! The old fellows who knew Paolo Vanni well, had some doubt upon this subject. Don Evandro, who knew him thoroughly well, had no doubt at all about it. It might have been in his power to induce his old parishioner and friend to come down with a part of his hoarded *scudi* to buy his son's freedom. But Don Evandro had no intention to do anything of the sort. He had more than one reason for not wishing that any part of old Paolo Vanni's money should be spent in such a manner. In the first place it would be lending aid and support to the heretical and accursed Italian government. Don Evandro, as has been said, was a keen politician. He was a priest of that class, which, while entirely giving up the world, in so far as making themselves before all things churchmen, and

having no interest, or ambition, or affection for
anything save the Church can be called giving
up the world, yet remain, to all spiritual interests
and purposes, intensely worldly. He was a sworn,
true, and loyal churchman, ready to sacrifice
much, to dare all things, and to deem all things
permissible for the service of the Church. But
of any other meaning of the term, save the
visible and bodily constitution of the great cor-
poration to which he belonged, he had about as
much idea as a Red Indian.

The curate of Santa Lucia intended, therefore,
that his parish should furnish as few men to Victor-
Emmanuel as might be. There were the hills near
at hand. There was no contending influence on
the spot to thwart his—no resident land-owners,
no gentry. He had always possessed a very
powerful influence over his—not all very poor, but
all very ignorant — parishioners ; and now he
meant to use it. It was necessary to be careful,
however. The government was on the watch ; it
knew very well that the priests were almost to a
man its enemies. Its suspicions were fully aroused ;
and the game to be played was not one altogether
without danger.

But the curato had in the special case of Beppo

Vanni a second reason for not choosing that he
should either serve his time in the army, or be
bought off by his father. He had thoroughly
espoused his old friend's cause in the matter of
Beppo's marriage. It was all in the line of his
own duty and scheme of conduct to secure Sandro
Bartoldi's money to the right side, instead of
allowing it to go entirely to swell the means of the
enemy, as would be the case if Lisa married Captain Brilli : not to mention that a match between
Giulia and Beppo might, as the priest shrewdly
guessed from all he had ever seen of Giulia, go far
to endanger the subserviency of the Vanni money
also to the good cause. It was therefore on all
accounts necessary that Beppo should marry Lisa,
and should not marry Giulia.

Those who live in a state of society in which
priestly influence has comparatively little power
over the secular affairs of private life, and which
is not divided into two utterly opposed parties by
any such broad line of demarcation as that which
separates Italian society into irreconcileably hos-
tile camps, can hardly appreciate at its real
importance the effects of such a system of
tactics, as that above indicated, carried out by so
powerfully an organised body as the Italian

clergy consistently, perseveringly, and unfail-
ingly.

Now, if Beppo went to serve his time, he would
come back with an additional prestige in Giulia's
eyes, utterly emancipated from priestly control,
and very probably in a great degree emancipated
from parental control also. His return might be
looked for at a fixed and known time, and there
was everything to encourage Giulia to wait for
him.

If, on the other hand, his father were induced
to conquer his avarice so far as to pay the sum
necessary to procure a substitute, he would remain
in the country free to continue his pursuit of
Giulia, and it would be very difficult to keep them
apart.

But if, on the contrary, old Paolo were coun-
selled to refuse to pay for a substitute,—counsel
which he would be only too ready to follow,—and
if Beppo should get a bad number, and could be
persuaded to go off to the hills, Victor-Emmanuel
would lose a first-rate soldier ; a contribution to
the general lawlessness, discontent, and ungovern-
ableness of the country would be achieved, and
Beppo would be effectually separated from Giulia ;
his return uncertain ; his entire future precarious

and full of difficulty; and possibly—who could tell?—old Paolo's succession secured to the much promising and well-disposed Carlo.

And what were the views of honest Beppo himself respecting this dreaded conscription? Unfortunately they were such as to render him but too easy a victim to the priest's designs, should he have the misfortune to be drawn to serve. Beppo was a thorough *contadino*, with all the feelings, all the prejudices, and all the ignorance of his class. The thought of being carried away from his native hills to some unknown and strange country, was intolerable to him. He had but very hazy and vague notions as to the nature of a soldier's life and duties. It was something, he knew, which men maimed and mutilated themselves to avoid—which men had before now killed themselves to avoid. For such stories of the desperation of the populations subjected to the remorseless conscription of Austria had reached those hills. He knew, or supposed he knew, that it involved monk-like self-abnegation, and entire subjection to the will of another in all things. None had ever, in the experience of these Romagnole rustics, left their country in compliance with the horrible conscription, and returned to their homes. None could have done so, for the conscription was now applied to that country for the first time. But in the absence of any such experience, all possibility of return was disbelieved. To be taken by the conscription was to bid a long adieu to all that made life precious, and to go forth into some unknown but terribly imagined state of misery and torment, never more to see the beloved hills, and yet more beloved faces of Romagna!

And even if he were to believe in the possibility of a return at some distant period, how could Beppo bear to tear himself away from Giulia, as matters stood with him? If she loved him, if she would only admit that he was dear to her, and he could think of her, while he was undergoing his terrible fate in some distant land, as safe at home, thinking of him, waiting for his return, and unexposed to the pursuit of others, the misery might be more tolerable. But, as it was, to leave her unwon, to leave her a mark for the admiration and pursuit and wooing of all the young men in Fano, and he far away the while, not knowing anything, but dreading all things respecting what was going on at home—this was absolutely intolerable to him. He could not face it.

So there was but a lottery chance between poor

Beppo and frantic desperation! If the chance were to go against him, the priest's suggestions would find him but too well prepared to listen to them.

As to the hope that his father would, if the bad chance hit him, sacrifice such a sum as would liberate him from it, he had little or no hope of that. He knew his father too well! And a Romagnole peasant has too great a veneration for money, and too vivid a sense of the difficulty of obtaining it, and of the amount of toil, patience, self-denial, and time which hoarded money represents, to blame his father in his heart for his avarice as severely as another might have done. In truth Beppo could have given the money to save himself, or to save one he loved; but he considered that in so doing he should have been reprehensible rather than otherwise, on the score of profusion and reckless extravagance. No! He had no expectation that his father would sacrifice money to buy him off his fate.

Little was known yet among the rural communes on the subject that was engrossing all their thoughts, except that the orders for making out the lists of those liable to serve had come, and that the lists were about to be made forthwith.

But this first step in the business involved no
action on the part of the victims, and no outward
and visible sign of the action of others. It was
completed silently in the bureaux of the authorities. It was like the first driving together of
a herd of wild cattle, destined to be afterwards
forced through some narrow pass, where the
hunters will pick them off as they rush by.
There was a vague knowledge among the herd
that they were being driven together, and that
was all as yet.

All was ignorance and doubt, and terror made
worse by these. A thousand different reports were
spread about the country. Some said it was only
a precautionary preparation, in case there should
be war with Austria, and might therefore never
come to anything. Some said that the drawing
was fixed for the following year; some, that it all
depended on the king's pleasure; some, that it
was all a chance ; some few, that it was a dreadful
certainty, and that the drawing was to be proceeded with directly.

Tormented by all this doubt and uncertainty,
Beppo determined to make it partly the real
motive, and partly the excuse, for a journey to
Fano. He fancied that his father had been less

willing than used to be the case, to allow him to go to the city. He used to go frequently on market days; but lately his father for two or three weeks past made excuses for keeping him at home; and upon one occasion during that time, when the business of the farm had required that somebody should go to Fano, the old man had chosen to go himself. Beppo understood very well that the purpose of all this was to keep him from seeing Giulia—very likely to make her think that he did not care to see her. But now his father could hardly object to his going to the city in a matter of such vital importance to himself. Poor Beppo was in truth very anxious to obtain some certainty upon the subject; but he was yet more anxious if possible to see Giulia, and ascertain how she was going on—whether she had already gathered a circle of admirers about her; whether she had made any acquaintances of any kind; whether she was turning into a fine town lady.

So, one evening as they were returning from the field, he broached the subject to his father, saying that he ought to make himself acquainted with the truth about the conscription.

Old Paolo admitted that, and said that he would consider what day he could best be spared from the farm; but his real object was to consult his spiritual adviser upon the point.

So, instead of lounging in the "loggia"—as he smoked his cigar, after supper, before going to bed—he strolled up to Santa Lucia, and saw the priest.

"Beppo has been telling me, your reverence, that he wants to go to Fano to learn about the conscription. I doubt me, he wants something else more!"

"No doubt, no doubt! I wonder you have been able to keep him quiet so long! Yes! let him go to Fano. It is right that he should learn all the particulars of the new law, since they touch him so nearly."

"He talks of going on Saturday."

Saturday was the Fano market-day, on which large numbers of the countrymen of the neighbouring districts (more of those from the surrounding plains, however, than of the hill people) were wont to assemble in the great piazza of the city.

"I am going in myself, on Saturday," replied the priest. "Suppose—or—no," he added, after a little meditation; "tell him that there is something to be done,—that you cannot well spare him on Saturday; but that he may go on the following day. I may just as well see Signor Sandro myself, and perhaps *la* Giulia, too, before he goes in."

Old farmer Vanni, who, in fact, scarcely ventured on an action, in any direction, without the advice and approbation of his friend Don Evandro, was, as is generally the case with hen-pecked husbands and priest-ridden laymen, specially unwilling to be thought to be guided by the *curato's* advice. So he said nothing that night in reply to his son's proposal; but while they were at their work the next morning, which was the Friday, he told him that he was loath that the hoeing of the bean-crop should be left till it was finished; rain might come—most likely would come—and then, where should they be? If he would stay tomorrow, and get the job finished, he should go to Fano on Sunday.

So it was settled that Beppo was to go into the city on the Sunday.

CHAPTER IV.

THE CHURCH OF THE OBSERVANTINES.

N THE Sunday morning, accordingly, Beppo started on his way to Fano. The priest had made his intended visit to the city on the Saturday, and had come home at night. But none of the Bella Luce family had seen him since his return. Beppo's heart beat fast as he found himself nearing the city; and, in his nervous impatience, he could not forbear from pushing on his horse to a speed that brought him to the end of his journey a good half-hour earlier than he had calculated on arriving. In the deadest and sleepiest of Italian cities there always is a little more stir and life on a Sunday than on other days. And this extra movement is not wholly ecclesiastical in its character. Sunday is the great day for recreation

and amusement of all kinds, not despite the
efforts of the clergy to make it otherwise, but
with their approval and sanction. But there are
various sorts of secular business, not partaking
in any degree of the nature of diversion, which
are apt to fall into the course of the Sunday's
occupations. It is naturally the day on which
the countrymen can most easily come into town.
Such shops as they may be likely to need are
apt to be open; and such business as may involve
interviews between them and the denizens of the
city are wont to be transacted.

Beppo, having put up his horse at the *osteria*
used by the *contadini* from his part of the country,
hurried to the house of Signor Sandro. From
him he could learn all he wanted to know about
the conscription, and from Lisa he doubted not
that he should be able to find out the whereabouts of the house in which his treasure was
lodged;—a circumstance of which he had as yet
been able to ascertain nothing;—for, of course,
neither his father nor Don Evandro were likely
to afford him any information upon this subject.
Indeed, Signor Paolo did not himself know where
the house of Giulia's mistress was situated.

It was about eleven o'clock when Beppo reached

the attorney's house. The little man was in his office ; and Beppo was told that he must wait in a passage, where three or four other countrymen, in their best Sunday attire, were already waiting, seated on a long bench against the wall, till their turn should come to be admitted to the attorney's presence.

Had they been townsmen, they would all, however much previously strangers to each other, have been in full conversation together. But being *contadini* they sate in silence, with care-worn anxious faces, but with meek-eyed patience, till the great authority sitting in that awful sanctum on the other side of the partition-wall should be ready to receive them, and give them the fatal answers of the oracle. But Beppo, in his anxiety, had raised his voice in speaking with the servant-girl, who had opened the door to him ; and the attorney, having overheard and recognised it, came hurrying out of his den with his pen in his hand.

" What, Signor Beppo ! Is it you ? What good chance is it brings *you* to Fano ? Delighted to see you, as we always are ! "

" There were two or three things, Signor Sandro—" began Beppo, slowly and timidly ; but the brisk little man cut him short.

"Look here, Signor Beppo!" he said, taking
him by the button, and drawing him a little down
the passage away from the men who were sitting
there, and dropping his voice to a whisper; "you
see how it is—all these people waiting to see me!
Never was so busy! All through this troublesome
conscription! Have not a minute to spare! But,
look here; come back at one, and eat a bit of
dinner with us. Poor Lisa will be *so* delighted to
see you; and I know your visit is more to her
than to me. Ah, you young fellows! Well, I
was young myself once! And then we shall have
leisure for a little talk. *A riveder—la!* At one,
mind! And Beppo," added the little man, standing on tiptoe to whisper in his ear, "Lisa is gone
to mass at the Church of the Servites. If you
should happen to fall in with her there, don't
tell her that I told you so."

And so saying he opened the door for his visitor,
and hurried back to the discussion of exemptions
and substitutes with his clients.

Beppo, with thus nearly two hours on his hands,
did not, despite his being utterly at a loss how to
get rid of them, feel much inclined to go to the
Servite Church. He wanted to have some conversation with Lisa, too. But the very evident hints

of Signor Sandro, to the effect that it was expected of him that he should make love to her, had the effect of making him feel shy. It takes so much to make an Italian of the cities feel shy and so little to produce that effect on one of the *conta-dino* class!

Beppo felt more inclined to spend his two hours in wandering through the city, to try if he could divine from the outward appearance of the houses which of them held his, Giulia. It seemed to his imagination an absurd and incredible thing that she should be behind any one of those walls or windows, and that no recognisable difference should exist in that wall or window—that there should be no *schekinah*, no outward and visible glory betokening the presence of such an inmate. He went mooning through the streets at hazard, gazing at the houses and windows wistfully, but without being able to obtain the slightest satis-faction from the investigation.

At length, having wandered into a part of the city far away from the attorney's house, he found himself in a quiet, utterly-deserted street, partly made up of dead walls. But on the opposite side to that on which he was standing, and a little in advance of him, there was a small church, and beyond that a very large and handsome palace. There was not a soul besides himself in the street ; but as he stood gazing down it, and doubting whether he should go any farther in that direction, which seemed to lead to the outskirts of the town among a wilderness of garden-walls and open spaces, he saw a party of people coming out of the little church, and beginning very slowly to descend the steps that led to the street.

They moved very slowly ; for the lady who came first was enormously fat : and though she had the arm of a young man to assist her—an officer of *Bersaglieri*, Beppo saw by his uniform, which, from a regiment of that branch of the service having been for some months stationed at Fano, was known to him—she came down the steps with some difficulty. But in the next moment all the blood in his body seemed to make a sudden rush to his heart, and there remain in a great frozen lump. Behind that enormous fat woman came—*la Giulia !* And—heavens and earth !—she had another of the same corps in attendance on her ; not an officer, but a corporal ! Yes, there was his stripe—a corporal of Bersaglieri ! Was it possible ? Could he believe his eyes ? He must be mistaken ! The beautiful

creature he was looking at, as if she had been a
Medusa, seemed more beautiful to his eyes than
ever. Was it Giulia? She was no longer dressed
altogether as a *contadina;* and though still wearing only a kerchief on her head, it was far more
coquettishly arranged than it used ever to be at
Bella Luce; and there were sundry other little
town-bred changes in her costume that seemed—
to the eyes which had the Bella Luce Giulia so
indefaceably photographed on their retina—to
make the present avatar very different from the
old one, though the worshipper could not deny
that it was one of enhanced glory. But was it
Giulia, or was he dreaming?

How exquisitely lovely, but yet how detestable
—how horrible was the vision! Who and what
was that horrid corporal—brisk, smart, tight
little man—who wore his round plumed hat in
the most jaunty manner? Corporals of Bersaglieri are all brisk, smart, tight little men, who
wear their hats in a jaunty manner. And he
danced and skipped by Giulia's side, chattering
and gesticulating, and looking up into her face;
and she was laughing, and looking as happy as a
queen. She had never laughed when *he* had
looked into her face. And now that disgusting

corporal! evidently a very witty and agreeable
corporal;—she was listening to all he said, and
evidently amused by it. She could have bounded
down the church-steps like one of the Bella Luce
goats, and so could the corporal of Bersaglieri too,
for that matter. But slow as the fat woman in
front of them was, they seemed to be in no hurry;
but stopped, and laughed, and sauntered on again,
clearly well pleased to linger over the matter as
long as might be.

Beppo, at the first moment of catching sight of
her, had thrown himself precipitately behind a
pillar by the side of a palace-door, on the side of
the street on which he was standing; and had
watched all the above dreadful spectacle, cautiously looking out from behind it. But, as he
bitterly said to himself, there was no danger of
her seeing him : she was far too much .occupied
by listening to that odious corporal!

But, once again, could it be Giulia? Or was it
possible that his eyes, even at the distance at
which he was, could see Giulia and doubt whether
it were really she, or not?

While he was still gazing out from behind his
shelter, with fixed stony eyes and open mouth,
the fat lady achieved the descent of the steps, and,

waddling along the pavement with the assist-
ance of the captain's arm, turned in at the grand
door of the palace next the church. Giulia—
if it was Giulia—and the corporal followed her ;
and Beppo was left staring after them, among the
people, who had by that time begun to leave the
church.

Surely it could not be that Giulia lived in such
a grand house as that ! Signor Sandro had spoken
of the lady, in whose service she was to live, as
by no means a rich person ;—a widow-lady, living
quite in a modest manner. It could not be that
that was her residence : he must have been mistaken ! Now the glorious yet hateful vision was
no longer before his eyes, he began to persuade
himself that it must have been a mistake—an
hallucination ! Yet, again—his head swam round !
—he was determined to know the worst. He had
already made a step or two across the street with
the intention of entering the alarmingly magnificent porch, in which the party he had seen had
vanished (captain, corporal, and all), when he was
arrested by the thought of how he was to accom-
plish his purpose. He must ring at the great
door ; when the servant came what was he to say ?
—ask if one Giulia Vanni lived there ? And if

the reply were in the affirmative, what then? His *contadino* timidity and shyness dared not thus beard the city magnificences. Besides, he should soon know all! There was another way. He would go at once to the Church of the Servites, and see if he could meet Lisa; if not, he should probably find her at home. From her he should be able to learn the truth.

So he asked one of the people who were coming from the church, from which the fat lady and her attendants had issued, and obtained a direction to the Servite church. The high mass was just over there also, by the time he reached it; and he had not watched at the door long before little Lisa, accompanied by her maid, came out. She looked so smart in her Sunday dress, that poor Beppo felt shy of accosting her there, in the street, amid all the people thronging out of the church. But the emergency was too pressing to admit of hesitation. So he stepped up to her, and instantly disobeyed her father's injunction by saying:

"Signorina, your father told me that I should most likely find you here. I came in from Bella Luce this morning."

" Oh, Signor Beppo! I am so glad to see you!

I have been thinking that you were never coming
to Fano any more! And yet—one would have
thought that you would have found more to do in
the city than ever! What on earth has become
of you? You have not come a bit too soon, I can
tell you."

"What do you mean, Signora Lisa?" replied
Beppo, while a cold sweat came over him. "Is
there—anything new?"

"*Altro!* You should not have stayed away so
long. Out of sight out of mind, you know!"

"May I walk home with you, Signorina? Your
father has kindly asked me to dine there. But I
came here because I was so anxious; and—I
knew that you would—tell me—tell me—all!"
faltered Beppo, whose words seemed to stick in
his throat as he uttered them.

"But first tell me why you have been so long
without coming to Fano? I thought, of course,
that you would have come in to see Giulia at least
every market-day. And I am sure she expected
it, too, though she has never said a word. And
in all this time you have never been near her
once."

"Because I could not! They would not let me
leave the farm. Oh, Signora Lisa! can you doubt

that I was anxious to come? But, now that I
have come, what am I the better? What can
I do? But do you know, Lisa," he continued,
dropping his voice to a shuddering whisper, "I
think I have seen her—I think I saw her in the
street this morning."

"Think you saw Giulia! Why, Signor Beppo,
what do you mean?" said Lisa, looking up at
him in amazement. "Don't you know whether
you saw her or not? Did you not speak to her if
you saw her?"

"No! I did not speak to her. I—I—I did
not feel certain—she seemed so changed. But
tell me first of all where she lives? Is it a very
large house?"

"Yes. The Pallazzo Bollandini; one of the
largest palaces in Fano!"

"Very grand?"

"Yes; a very fine house."

"And is it next door to a church?" asked
Beppo, in increasing agony, while his great
stalwart legs seemed to tremble under him.

"Yes, it *is* next door to the Church of the
Observantines. Why, what of it?"

"And is—the lady she is living with a very
stout woman?" asked he, still hoping against

hope, and longing to hear that Giulia's mistress was by no means particularly stout.

But Lisa ruthlessly destroyed the last gleam of hope.

"Yes, *la* Signora Dossi *is* a *very* stout woman," she said.

"Then it is all over with me!" said Beppo, in a voice of the deepest despair; "there can never be anything again between me and Giulia!"

"What do you mean, Signor Beppo? All over between you and Giulia, because Signora Dossi is very fat! What can you mean? I do not understand you this morning! If it was after dining with papa, instead of before——"

(The Romagnoles are not marked to the same degree by that exemplary sobriety which distinguishes the Tuscans.)

"I am sober enough, *pur troppo!*" returned Beppo, with intense sadness in his voice. "Then I *did* see Giulia, just now. She was coming out of a church with a monstrously fat woman, and they went into an enormous palace next door."

"Well! and why did you not speak to her?"

"Lisa," said Beppo, in a low voice of the deepest tragedy, "Lisa, there was a corporal with her!"

"Ah, the corporal!" said Lisa, in a voice which

indicated that the corporal was no new pheno-
menon to her.

" Lisa ! "

" And who was with the fat lady ? " asked Lisa,
rather hurriedly.

" The fat lady had hold of the arm of a captain
of Bersaglieri."

" Dear me ! I wonder what o'clock it is ! " said
Lisa. " I wonder whether there could be time.
We don't dine till one, and cook is always a
quarter of an hour behindhand."

" Time for what, Signorina Lisa ? It is striking the quarter to one, now, by the clock in the
piazza. Oh, Lisa ! I am very miserable ! " said
poor Beppo, in a tone which seemed to convey a
little reproach for the manner in which she had
received his communication of the misfortune of
the corporal.

" Time to go and see—Giulia before dinner.
I was thinking we could go together, and pay a
visit to Signora Dossi ; but I am afraid we have
not time," she added, with a voice of much disappointment.

" Me ! I could not think of doing such a
thing ! " said Beppo, with terror and horror in his
voice.

"What! not go and see Giulia!"

"With that corporal there!" shuddered Beppo.

"Oh! the corporal is only with Captain Brilli. That was Captain Brilli that you saw with *la* Signora Dossi," said Lisa, blushing a little, and laughing a little more.

"Oh—h—h! Ah—h—h!" rejoined Beppo, with a varying intonation that marked the progressive development of enlightenment in his mind; "that is why you would go there. But, Signora Lisa, I can't go there to see that corporal and Giulia together. It would make me mad!"

"But that is just the reason you should go there, Signor Beppo," reasoned little Lisa. "Perhaps, if you had not stayed away from Fano so long, the corporal would not have had so good a chance. But take my word for it, Giulia don't care a fig for him. He *does* go on with her, to be sure. And he is a very amusing man, the corporal. And what is a poor girl to do?—and such a girl as Giulia is, too! How can you think that she is to live in a town like Fano,—specially when the place is full of officers and soldiers,—and not be admired and run after?"

Poor Beppo groaned deeply. "How long has she known the man?" he asked, despondingly.

"Oh ! Captain Brilli goes very often to *la* Dossi. I hardly ever can see him anywhere else to speak to him. And Corporal Tenda is very much with him. I believe the corporal * at home in Pied-mont is rather above his position in the army. He is a very respectable sort of man, I fancy. And so he made acquaintance with Giulia, you see. And how could she help it ? But I don't believe she cares a bit about him,—not to say, really care," pleaded Lisa.

But Beppo had seen the corporal's manner and his look, as he seemed, to Beppo's imagination, to surround her on all sides at once with his accursed agile assiduity ; he had seen the attention Giulia was according to him, and had observed the merry laughing intelligence in her eye. He had con-trasted with this his own physical and mental atti-tude when near her, and her manner towards him ; and the iron had entered into his soul !

* It may be observed, also, that the social distance between an officer and a non-commissioned officer is very much less in the Italian Army than in our own.

CHAPTER V.

CORPORAL TENDA.

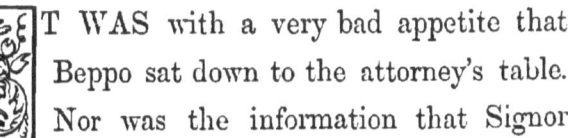T WAS with a very bad appetite that Beppo sat down to the attorney's table. Nor was the information that Signor Sandro had to communicate to him respecting the other great object of his visit to the city at all more consoling to him than that which had already made life seem not worth having to him since that morning. If the conscription had simply involved getting knocked on the head and put out of his pain at once, he felt as if he could have been quite contented to draw Number One!

The news which the attorney had to give him, indeed, confirmed all the worst fears of the poor fellows whom he left at Santa Luce, anxiously awaiting the tidings that he would bring back from the city. The conscription was not merely threatened; it was certain. It was not for next year, but for this. The day for the drawing had not been appointed for Fano yet; but it would be very shortly known, and would certainly be not longer than a fortnight after the completion of the communal lists. His brother Carlo was exempt; but he, Beppo, was as surely liable as any man in the district;—"and it is not very easily that they will let a fellow of your inches out of their clutches, my friend, if you once get into them," added the attorney.

"One can but take one's chance!" said Beppo, striving to put the best face on the matter that he could. "After all, the chance is in one's favour."

"Well, yes, as far as equal chances go, it's in your favour, of course; but the devil of it is that these *signori uffiziali* are bent upon getting the likeliest men. And if the draft were for a hundred, say, and you drew number two hundred, I should be sorry to insure you!"

"Why, how can that be, Signor Sandro? If a man is not fairly drawn, he cannot be taken, I suppose?"

"Aha! fairly drawn! That's all very well!

But it is not every man who is fit to serve! There is the medical examination! Ever so many are sure to be rejected! Then, as I tell you, they make all sorts of excuses to reject the smaller and weaker men, in order to get a chance of laying hold of a fellow like you. I suppose you can't make out that you have got anything the matter with you?" said the attorney, with a laugh.

"Oh, yes, he has!" put in little Lisa; "he has got a sore heart; and I am sure that is a very bad complaint. He has a very sore heart ever since I have been telling him all about *la* Giulia!"

"Oh, if that's his complaint, it's likely enough to get worse instead of getting better," said the attorney, affecting to give a low whistle, and turn his eyes up to the ceiling, as if that was a dull matter, about which the less was said the better.

"Why, what is there to be said against *la* Giulia?" said Beppo, almost fiercely.

"Against her? Oh, nothing! nothing at all! I never say anything against anybody. But it may be that all the world is not equally prudent or equally indulgent."

"Come now, papa," said Lisa, "you know there is nothing to be said against poor Giulia, at all.

Of course it cannot be expected that such a girl as Giulia should not be admired!"

"Well, it may be so, of course. And some men may have no objection to take up with a girl who has been flirted with by half the town, and talked of by the whole of it. Others may not like it. It's a matter of taste. If I was a young fellow in a respectable and good position, the head of my family—to be so one day, at least—and looked up to by all the country, I should not like to make a girl my wife who had gone through that sort of thing. Girls are easily spoilt;—and the handsomest perhaps the quickest."

"Tell me the truth, now, as an old friend, Signor Sandro!" said Beppo, piteously, while the big drops of perspiration gathered on his brow; "do you mean that *la* Giulia has got herself talked about in a way—that—that a good girl should not?"

"Well, my dear friend, it is a difficult question to answer! It is hard to say what a good girl may do, and what she may not. I don't wish to be severe. I dare say *la* Giulia is a very good girl, as girls in her position are,—a very good girl. But she has been very much—admired, we will say. She has been a good deal spoken of.

Men *will* speak of such things in a tone like this. No doubt *la* Giulia has had her head turned a little! *Che vuole?* No doubt it would have been better if she had kept this Corpoal Tenda— I think they call him—more at a distance. Still there is no great harm in it all! Only that if I, as a man who has some knowledge of the world, and as an old friend of the family, were asked for my advice in the matter of choosing a wife for your father's son,—why, I should not pitch upon Giulia Vanni. Girls of her sort make the most charming sweethearts in the world. But a good wife is another sort of article!"

Beppo knew perfectly well that the attorney had a motive for saying all this. He knew perfectly well what that motive was. Nevertheless it gave him exquisite pain to hear it. Did not what had fallen from Lisa, who had no such motive, but quite the contrary, confirm it? Worse than all, did not the evidence of his own eyes vouch for the truth of a good deal of it? He dreaded, yet longed for, an interview with her. If only he could have heard her disculpate herself! He would believe every word she said. That he was quite determined on. Did Giulia ever lie? He would believe her in preference to all the calumnious tittle-tattle tongues in the city. If only she would say that—that—that—she loved him, Beppo Vanni, in short; that was, in point of fact, the exculpation that he thirsted to hear from her own lips!

Signor Sandro, if he had effected nothing else by his insinuations, had effectually destroyed the convivial capabilities of his guest. Beppo sat moody and silent, and could not be induced to drink, when the cheese and fruit were placed upon the table. The attorney made one or two hospitably-meant attempts to induce him to do so, but finding it of no avail, he said:

" Well, Signor Beppo, if you will not drink any more wine, I shall take my *siesta*. If you like to do the same, make yourself at home. And if you like to take Lisa to the *passeggiata* after-wards, I have no doubt she will be well pleased. You will find me in my study when you come back; and if you will look in for a moment before you mount, I will give you a line to take to your good father from me. *A riveder la !* "

As soon as ever Lisa and Beppo were left alone together, Lisa said:

" Now, Beppo, you must not mind a word of all papa was saying. It is all stuff and nonsense.

You know what he has got in his head,—more
stuff and nonsense still. Don't you believe a word
of it!"

"But when I saw that corporal with my own
eyes, Lisa!"

"Saw the corporal! What of that? Do you
think Giulia is going to shut herself up as if she
was a nun, for you; and you never to come near
her for weeks and weeks? But, I tell you she
don't care a fig's end for the corporal! Just you
see her, and it will all come right!"

"How am I to see her, Lisa?" asked Beppo, in
a very piteous tone.

"How? Why come to *la* Dossi's house, now
directly, with me, to be sure!"

"Oh, Lisa! and if that corporal is still there?"

"That is just what you must go for, Signor
Beppo. You must go and see for yourself that
there is nothing at all serious between Giulia
and Corporal Tenda. And, besides that, you
must go, to let Giulia know that you are thinking
of her. You have stayed away too long. What
do you suppose Giulia would feel if she heard
that you had been to Fano, and gone away without so much as making any attempt to see her!
I know what I should feel if Captain Brilli treated

me in such a way. Why, she would be justified
in taking up with the corporal or anybody else
out of sheer despair, she would. Most likely,"
continued Lisa, improving upon the idea which
had only that instant come into her head for the
first time, "most likely it's merely *that* which
has led her to encourage the corporal at all,—if
she has encouraged him, which I, for one, don't
believe. But you must not think that if you
don't do your duty by poor Giulia, the corporal
won't make the most of it to her. Of course he
will. And small blame to him! If he should
hear—as of course he will hear—that you have
been to Fano, and never been near her, he will
make a pretty story of it to her;—and then—
there's no saying what a girl may do in such a
case as that!"

We know that little Lisa had her own reasons
for being determined to pay a visit that afternoon,
while her father was enjoying his siesta, to her
friend, Signora Dossi. Nevertheless, it cannot be
denied that her arguments were sound; unless,
indeed, Beppo were minded to give up the matter
altogether; and once or twice the vision of that
corporal at Giulia's side, on the church-steps, and
of her manner, as she listened to him, as it re-

curred to his mind, almost made him wish to do so. The words of Signor Sandro, too, had not been without their effect, even though he knew that the counsel given was interested. For the well-to-do *contadino* is very sensitive to the voice of his public in matters of the sort. It would *not* be well for Vanni of Bella Luce to take home a wife who had been the town-talk of all Fano! That was true, let what would be the attorney's motive for saying it. It was true! and he was mad, and miserable, and infatuated! He could not give up Giulia, however much his reason might be convinced that it were better that he should do so. He *could* not do it. Give her up! He knew at the bottom of his heart, all the time that he was irresolutely hesitating whether he should consent to go with Lisa or not, that he would rather give up his life than give her up. And then he thought over all the incidents —the things spoken and the things done—under the cypress-tree, in the path between Bella Luce and Santa Lucia ; and his anger was forgotten, and his heart yearned towards her ; and he would forgive her everything—if only she would be forgiven !

" Come, Signor Beppo !—come along ! You

can, at all events, come with me as far as the
door of Palazzo Bollandini. We can talk of
your going in or not by the way. Any way, it's
as well to be walking as sitting here. Come
along!"

So—merely out of civility to *la* Lisa, and because he could not help himself, he put on his
hat and accompanied her.

It had seemed to Beppo in the morning that
the Palazzo Bollandini was a long way off from
Signor Sandro Bartoldi's house—very much further
than it now appeared! Perhaps he had not come
the shortest way in the morning. Perhaps the
difference was due to the different attitude of
his own mind. He had made very small progress
towards determining what he would do when he
got there, when he found himself with Lisa before the huge portal of the palace; and he
recognised, with a shudder, the church front and
the steps where that horrid vision of Giulia and
the Bersaglieri corporal had blasted his eyes.

Lisa entered the great gateway, and tripped up
the huge staircase without pausing a second to
give Beppo time to think what he should do.
She skipped up the stairs to the *primo piano*,
and he had nothing for it but to run up after

her. She seized the little bit of scarcely visible twine—knowing right well exactly where to look for it—while he was lost in awe and wonderment at the grandeur of the place he had entered, and rang as vigorous a peal as the little bell-pull would execute.

"But, Signora Lisa," remonstrated Beppo; "I think——"

But they had not to wait for the opening of the door so long this time as when Giulia and Signor Sandro had stood before it, for they were lighter feet which went across the huge hall to admit them.

While Beppo's hesitating remonstrances were yet on his lips, the door was opened by Giulia herself.

It was of course the most natural thing in the world that it should be so ; but the possibility of it had never entered into Beppo's head for an instant. Probably the truth was, that he hardly realised the fact that that huge and magnificent door was absolutely the private entrance to the dwelling in which Giulia resided, but rather had an idea that a whole nest of homes would be found within it, in the furthermost penetralia of some one of which she would be at length reached.

And when the tall door opened, there, framed in the marble door-case, stood before him the figure of his enchantress, more beautiful than ever, set off with a hundred little town coquetries, —transmuted, glorified, but still unmistakeably the Giulia whose eyes had made the Bella Luce light deserve its name, and whose absence made all dark there. He was as much taken aback and rooted to the spot with speechless amazement as if he had suddenly met her at the antipodes.

He certainly had never seen her look so beautiful as she looked at that moment; and all—his own bitter agony, and the stinging insinuations of the attorney—would have been forgotten and forgiven on the spot, but for a withering sight that met his eyes as they looked beyond her into the space of the huge hall. There, immediately behind her, stood the odious, the intolerable corporal. He had evidently either been alone with her in the hall, or stuck to her so inseparably that he had accompanied her across it to open the door.

Beppo's eyes glared with rage and indignation·; and assuredly his whole appearance was very little like that of one meeting an old friend, to say nothing of an old love, with pleasure.

Giulia, too, was to a certain degree moved, and to a certain degree embarrassed by the presence of the corporal at her skirts. But when was ever a woman embarrassed under circumstances of the kind, let their difficulty be what it may, as a man is embarrassed.

Giulia's blood rushed to her face and neck, but she did not lose for an instant either her faculty of speech, or her presence of mind; nor did her voice shake, as she said:

"Ah, Signora Lisa! *Buon giorno! buona festa!* We have been expecting you!"

(Lisa stood nearest to the door, and Beppo's tall figure was seen over and behind her; therefore it was natural to address her first.)

"*Buon giorno*, Signor Beppo! Are they all well at Bella Luce? We did *not* expect to see you to-day."

Lisa had at once stepped into the hall; and was greeting the corporal in the style of an old acquaintance, leaving Giulia face to face with Beppo, who was still standing gaping, and almost gasping, on the landing-place outside the doorway.

"Signor Caporale," said she, turning to the corporal, after she had paused half-a-minute with the door in her hand, waiting for Beppo to enter, "will you have the kindness to await my cousin Beppo Vanni's decision whether he will come in or not. I must go and take *la* Signorina Lisa to *la padrona*."

And so saying she turned away to cross the hall, leaving Beppo and the corporal face to face. Lisa tried to throw an encouraging and inviting glance to poor Beppo, over her shoulder; but was obliged to hurry off with Giulia across the hall.

Beppo had a very good mind to turn on his heel without saying a word, shake the dust off his feet as a testimony against the abominable house he was in, and turn his back on it and Giulia for ever! Forgive her? No! he never, never could forgive her! It was monstrous! It was loathsome!

He had a very good mind to turn his back and walk away,—but he did not do it. For it was beyond his power.

"So you are Signor Beppo Vanni, are you? Come in, comrade, come in! the more the merrier!" said Corporal Tenda, after the two men had remained staring at each other for a minute without speaking;—Beppo looking scared

and savage, and the corporal perfectly self-possessed
and perfectly good-humoured.

Corporal Tenda was a model corporal of Bersaglieri, small, light-made, wiry, active, with a
shrewd, good-tempered, bright, sunburnt face, a
frank, bold blue eye, and a bush of short, crisp,
curly brown hair;—a dangerous man for a rival
in the good graces of a high-mettled girl, though
not comparable either in face or in person to the
handsome, stalwart, classical-featured Romagnole.
But if his limbs were nimbler than those of the
Herculean-proportioned Beppo, his wit was far
more so. A ready wit is not generally the distinguishing characteristic of the Piedmontese; and
Corporal Tenda was a native of that province;
doubtless of a stock deriving its origin as well as
its name from the little mountain village which
gives its well-known appellation to the picturesque
Alpine pass between Nice and Turin. The corporal was, as Lisa had said,—and as has been
by no means an uncommon case since Italy has
needed all her stoutest arms and hearts in the
ranks of her defenders—of a social position in his
own country somewhat higher than that which he
held (only provisionally, the corporal trusted) in
the army. He was a man of some little educa-

tion, of far more than poor Beppo could boast; and was, though a Piedmontese, a sharp, clever fellow. He was, moreover, a thoroughly good, honest-hearted little man; and though he had abundance of the military tendency to look down on the entire race of bumpkins, and quite a sufficiency of the provincial Piedmontese assumption of superiority to the inhabitants of the other provinces of Italy, yet any man who came into relationship of any kind with Corporal Tenda, and showed himself in that relationship to be a man of honour and character, was sure to be treated by him as he deserved.

"You know my name, then?" said Beppo, who had so far obeyed the corporal's invitation as to come just sufficiently far across the door-sill as to make it possible for the latter to close the door behind him. He had done so because he did not know what else to do. And now he stood moodily measuring his smart little enemy from head to foot, thinking how easy it would be to pitch him out of one of those great windows into the street, and how much he should like to do it. It no more came into his head to be personally afraid of the corporal, than he would have been of a little terrier who barked at his heels. But he was

much afraid of his uniform. The *contadino* mind
stands in great and habitual awe of the military.
For all that, Beppo would have been very glad to
pick a quarrel with him; though he had a vague
idea that to strike or resist such an embodiment
of the *forza pubblica* would *ipso facto* subject
him to be shot kneeling on his own coffin. But
he felt as if he should rather like to be kneeling
on his coffin than not, especially if Giulia could be
compelled to witness his fate, and to know that
he had incurred it by fighting to defend her from
all snares, corporals, and other emissaries of the
evil one. But Corporal Tenda did not seem to
intend to give him any opportunity of entering
on such a desperate course of conduct.

"Know your name, Signor Vanni!" said he
"*Altro!* I should think so, *per Bacco!* Who
does not know the name of Vanni?' Your lord-
ship shares it with the divinest girl in all Romagna
—in all Italy, I should say!"

"My business here was to see my cousin
Giulia," said Beppo, scowling more blackly than
ever. "My father is in some sort responsible for
—for her safety—and—and the decency of her
conduct."

"Ha! You come armed with parental autho-

rity, eh ? " and the corporal winked in the most
provokingly intelligent manner and the most
perfect good humour as he spoke. " Pray walk
in, and permit the Signorina Giulia to crave
your blessing. It will be, I doubt not, supremely
satisfactory to her ! Allow me to do the honours
of this poor mansion !" continued the corporal,
waving his hand, as he spoke, with the mock
airs of a host, and bowing low to Beppo as he
motioned him to precede him.

" My cousin is but a poor servant in this house,"
growled Beppo, while his mind was distracted
from what he was saying by a desire rapidly
becoming uncontrollable to spring on the accursed
corporal, and strangle him then and there. " If
she is disengaged, I might speak a few words to
her before I leave the city ; if not, it does not
matter,—not the least in the world. Perhaps I
had better not disturb her !"

" *Come ! vi pare !* Can you dream of it ? A
nice kind of guardian and protector you are for
a young girl. Oh—é, Signora Giulia !" he cried
out, raising his voice till it echoed again in the
large empty hall ; " here's Signor Beppo yearning
to give you his fatherly blessing ; but he is in
such a hurry just now to be off, that, if you do

not come out for it directly, he will carry it off straight back to the hills with him. Oh—é, Signora Giulia!"

"Hush—h—h!" cried Giulia, running out from the inner rooms, and holding up her hand with a warning gesture; "are you mad, Signor Caporale, to make such a noise as that? Don't you know that *la padrona* is taking her *siesta?*"

La padrona was taking her *siesta!* And Giulia had been alone, then, with this animal of a profligate corporal! thought Beppo to himself. It was too bad—too barefaced! Thank God he had come into the city, and made himself acquainted with the truth! Thank God he had escaped wrecking his heart on a worthless girl! Escaped? Poor Beppo groaned inwardly as the word returned to his mind in the guise of a question.

They had not been absolutely *tête-à-tête*, however, he thought. For he supposed that Captain Brilli must be in the house somewhere. Lisa had vanished into the inner penetralia, and no doubt knew of the captain's whereabouts.

The fact was, that the attorney's daughter and her lover were at that instant discussing all the chapter of their hopes and fears in a delicious *tête-à-tête* in *la* Dossi's vacant sitting-room.

"How could I think about *siestas* or anything else, when your estimable guardian here was talking of leaving the house without seeing you, gentilissima Signora Giulia?" said the corporal, adding action with both hands, as he stood a few yards from Beppo on the paved floor of the vast hall, and affecting to speak in a voice of urgent remonstrance.

"My guardian!" said Giulia, tossing her head.

"I made no such claim," said Beppo, sulkily; "I should be very sorry to assume such an office."

"Come to see that the young lady conducted herself decently, on behalf of her family, if I understand your worship aright," said the corporal, skipping into a new rhetorical attitude as he spoke.

"I said," replied Beppo, stammering and turning very red, "that—my father—and mother—would—would be glad to hear that my cousin Giulia was—was—was going on well. I leave it to her to judge how far they will be satisfied with my report!"

Giulia's eyes flashed at this, and the lightning was instantaneously followed by the thunderbolt.

"There is nobody at Bella Luce," she said, "to whom my conduct is of the slightest importance.

There is one way only in which I could grieve
the heart of Signor Paolo Vanni, and in that
way he may rest very sure I shall *never* afflict
him !"

Corporal Tenda saw with undisguised admiration, and Beppo with an agony made up of a sense
of self-blame conflicting with burning indignation
and ardent love for his cousin, how much scorn
could look beautiful in Giulia's eyes as she spoke
those last words—words which Beppo but too well
understood.

" *Diavolo !* If family matters of delicacy have
to be discussed—if the lady has confidences to
make to her father confessor, allow me to suggest
the privacy of a confessional !" said the corporal,
waving his hand towards the old sedan-chair in a
distant corner of the hall ! " it would be impossible
to desire better accommodation for the purpose."

" Don't be a fool, Signor Caporale," said Giulia,
as gravely as she could, but darting a laughing
glance out of the corner of her eye at the corporal,
as she spoke, which Beppo caught *in transitu*,
and which formed perhaps the heaviest item in all
the long bill against her scored up in his much-
lacerated heart. "If you choose to walk in,
Signor Beppo," she continued, in a milder tone,

though still very haughty—for she had been grievously offended by that ill-judged slip of the tongue which poor Beppo had been guilty of in the excess of his embarrassment and ill-humour in speaking to the corporal, and which the latter had so remorselessly turned to the utmost account —"if you choose to walk in I shall be happy to present you to *la* Signora Dossi, as soon as she wakes."

She spoke coldly and haughtily; but there was a feeling at her heart, due perhaps in some degree to the intensity of the misery which was legible in Beppo's handsome face, which prompted her to accompany her words with a look—not precisely of tenderness, and still less of pleading; but certainly of reconciliation and invitation. It was but momentary, however, and Beppo was either too slow to see it or too angry to heed it.

"I do not see that I could be of any use in coming in," said he, gloomily; "I should only interfere with the pleasant party assembled here. Besides, I must be starting for Bella Luce, and I can easily understand that you are in no hurry for *la* Signora Dossi to wake!"

The last words were accompanied by a look of indignant and bitter reproach at Giulia.

"As you please, Signor Beppo!" said she, at
once turning on her heel, and going towards the
door of the inner rooms; "Signor Caporale,"
she added, as she crossed the hall, "will you
kindly open the door for my cousin? I wish you
a pleasant ride home, Signor Beppo!"

And with those words she vanished; and instantly an immense and poignant repentance of
his refusal of her invitation fell upon Beppo.
He felt as if he would have given worlds to recall
it, if only for the gratification of his burning
curiosity to know what would pass between her and
the corporal during the remainder of *la* Dossi's
siesta,—if only to protect her, ungrateful as she
was, against that base and unprincipled wretch.
Protect her! How could he protect her? He
away at Bella Luce, and she with evidently all
sorts of opportunities of meeting him as often as
she pleased. And was he not already on terms of
intimacy with her such as Beppo had never been
able to attain, and that in a few weeks? and he
had worshipped her, and lived under the same
roof with her for years.

He turned slowly towards the door, with a hell
of contending passions seething in his heart,
—rage, bitter self-contempt, indignation, hatred,

horrible jealousy, and desperate and unquenchable love.

Yes, love, after all, through all, and above all. He told his heart that he despised her, and cast her off, and hated her ; and his heart knew that he lied, and loved her at the very moment as desperately as ever.

" Well, don't look so black about it, friend Beppo," said the corporal as he opened the door for him. " It seems that the young lady does not value the paternal blessing so much as I had supposed. Try her another way, next time."

" I want no next time," said Beppo. "It is not likely that I shall trouble your fun here another time."

" Well, we must try not to break our hearts. I won't answer for mine, for it's a very tender one," said the corporal, placing his hand on the organ in question, and bowing low as Beppo passed the door. "I dare say we shall meet again, though, for all that," he added, looking with a soldier's eye after Beppo as he went slowly down the great staircase ; " meantime, *buon viaggio, à rivederlo.*"

And Corporal Tenda shut the door after him with undiminished good humour.

It is so easy for a man to keep his good temper under such circumstances.

Beppo walked away through the streets, now filling with people in their holiday trim, for it was just the hour of the *passeggiata*, feeling as if he had been stunned and was reeling. He never thought of returning to Signor Sandro's house for the letter the attorney had asked him to carry to his father; but found his way somehow or other unconsciously to the *osteria* at which he had left his horse, and ordered it to be brought out to him with a manner and voice that made the lame ostler, whose lameness had recently become so valuable a possession, say to a bystander, as he rode off: "There's another that's been baulked in his hopes of getting a substitute. Wait awhile, and you'll see plenty more faces like that in Fano !"

Beppo let his nag choose his own pace, and find his own way back to Bella Luce. The old horse had no doubt on either point. He quietly sauntered along the well-known road, and never disturbed his master's deep reverie till he came to a full stop at his own stable-door.

The lights seemed to be all out in the farmhouse; for it was much beyond the usual bedtime of the inmates. Beppo, still moving as if in a dream, put his horse into the stable, took off his saddle ; and then, after standing awhile gazing sadly into the distant moonlight far down the valley, heaved a deep sobbing sigh, and turning away from the house towards the path leading to the village, walked straight to the great half-way cypress in the middle of the path.

There he flung himself on the turf at his length, and burst, great strong man as he was, into a passionate fit of tears.

When these had in some degree calmed the storm that was raging in his heart and brain, he set himself to think over every word, every accent, every gesture of the last meeting on that spot between him and Giulia. He would fain have found some motive of excuse, some possibility of explanation, from the comparison of her words and conduct then with what he had seen and heard that day. But each well-remembered look and phrase seemed to him only to make her present conduct appear the more odious, the more hideously inconsistent. False, false, false, as hell ! "No love, no love !" she had cried in the bitterness of her heart. "I *hate* them ! I hate all men !"

Oh, what a wreath of bitter, bitter scorn sate on Beppo's usually inexpressive lips, as he recalled the words!

All thought of the conscription seemed to have gone far, far away into the background, as if it appertained to some distant matter; but still his mind would go over and over again the scene of that last night; and still the tender feelings which, despite his reason, would fill his eyes with tears at the thoughts of it, were alternated with the hot fit of burning rage and shame, and scathing jealousy, as he recalled those other memories of the morning.

And so passed the hours, till the morning Ave Maria from the tower of the neighbouring church of Santa Lucia recalled him to the necessity of reporting himself at home, and commencing with his father and brother the morning's task.

CHAPTER VI.

DON EVANDRO AT WORK.

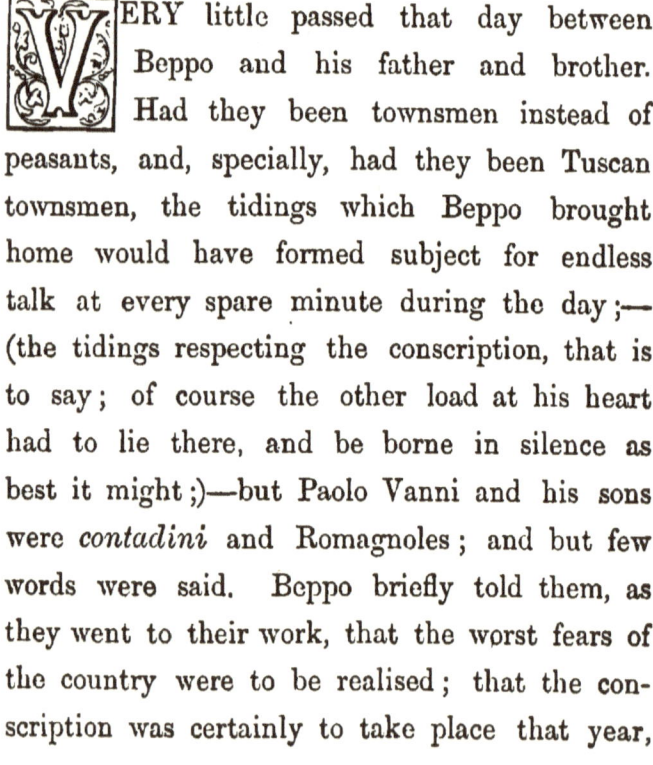

ERY little passed that day between Beppo and his father and brother. Had they been townsmen instead of peasants, and, specially, had they been Tuscan townsmen, the tidings which Beppo brought home would have formed subject for endless talk at every spare minute during the day;—(the tidings respecting the conscription, that is to say; of course the other load at his heart had to lie there, and be borne in silence as best it might;)—but Paolo Vanni and his sons were *contadini* and Romagnoles; and but few words were said. Beppo briefly told them, as they went to their work, that the worst fears of the country were to be realised; that the conscription was certainly to take place that year,

and that a day for the drawing would be named
shortly after the completion of the communal
lists.

At dinner-time the same information was given
in similarly concise words to the poor mother, who
manifested but little more emotion outwardly
than the male members of the family had done ;
but she rose early next morning, and privately
taking from the secret hoard of the produce of
her yarn, the price of two fair wax tapers of
half-a-pound each, she stole off to the village,
and, having bought what she needed, set them
up alight before the altar of the Blessed Virgin
of the Seven Sorrows, with an earnestly breathed
prayer that the holy Mother would deign, in
consideration of that humble offering, to preserve
a mother's son to her. True, all the other
mothers in the parish would, in all probability,
do the like. But it was not probable that any
one of them would go to the expense of tapers
of half-a-pound each. It was to be presumed,
therefore, that the prayer so backed would be
effectual. Nevertheless, poor Sunta, in her
anxiety, turned back when she had gone a few
steps from the church, and again kneeling before
the figure with the seven daggers, stuck in

artistic grouping through the satin of her stiffly brocaded, pyramidal-shaped robe, she promised two more tapers of equal size in case of a favourable result.

Poor mother! If earnestness could avail to make her prayer heard, it must have had its effect.

And so the day passed sombrely enough among the inhabitants of Bella Luce. The days had passed more sombrely there, even to old Paolo himself, since Giulia had left the farm. But that Black Monday, after Beppo's return from the city, was more so than ordinary.

In the evening, a little before supper-time, came Don Evandro. The priest was always a welcome guest at Bella Luce, for he knew how to make himself agreeable, with the tact so specially the gift of the Roman Catholic clergy, both to the farmer and to his wife. And the frequent presence of the priest at their table conferred a tone and style in the estimation of the Santa Lucia *beaumonde* that nothing else could have compensated for. Many of the parish clergy in the poorer and remoter districts of Italy are glad enough to give the consideration bestowed by their presence in return for the hospitality afforded them. But this was not Don Evandro's object. He was too well off, though far from being a rich man, to need a meal; and he had always some ulterior object in view. Power was what he wanted, and the means of leading his parish whithersoever he chose that it should go.

He was perfectly aware of Beppo's journey to Fano,—had in some degree prepared for it beforehand; and the object of his present visit to Bella Luce was to shape and confirm the impressions which he pretty shrewdly guessed the young man had brought back with him.

" I suppose, Signor Beppo, you brought home with you full information respecting this detestable and abominable conscription ? "

" Yes, your reverence. It seems that it is all determined on," said Beppo, in a weary and dispirited manner.

" And that is what the godless, usurping government and the infidel revolutionists call liberty ! Liberty !—the forcible tearing of the flower of the population from their homes and their families ! Man-stealers ! My heart bleeds for the unfortunates who are thus sent off to destruction, temporal and eternal. Ay, eternal ! For what are they when they come back to their

native soil,—if ever they do come back? Reprobates! They leave their paternal roofs well-disposed, God-fearing youths; and the few who ever
return are lost reprobates, fearing neither God
nor devil, filled with false notions and heresies,
perverted in heart and in mind alike. Were I
a father, I would rather see my son in his coffin
than see him taken by the accursed conscription."

The father and mother and the two sons
listened to this outburst with awe and terror.
And the old farmer began to fear that he should
certainly be expected to turn out his hoards, in
order to buy his son off destruction, temporal and
eternal.

"It is a very bad business," said the old man,
scratching his head; "I don't see what is to be
done in it—not I! Suppose our Beppo should be
drawn, your reverence; what can a poor man like
me do?"

"But there is good hope he may not be drawn;
surely there is good hope," said Signora Sunta,
clasping her hands. "The Holy Virgin is very
good. We have always done our best both at
Nativity and Conception, besides a candle at the
Annunciation—and always the best wax. Your
reverence well knows we have never failed," said

poor Sunta, appealingly; "surely we may hope that the Virgin will send us a good number."

"You have every reason, my dear friend, to expect a blessing on you and yours. I know nobody in whose case I should look forward to one with greater confidence," replied the priest; "but the worst of the misfortune is, that a good number cannot be trusted to as an escape."

"Signor Sandro told me something of that," said Beppo; "but I did not rightly understand him. He seemed to say, as far as I could make out, that after they had drawn the men by lot, if they did not like what the lot gave them, they picked out others."

"Well, it comes to nearly that," returned the priest ; "for these sons of Belial are not honest even in the carrying out of their own infamous laws. If there is a man they fancy anywhere near on the list, they will make all kinds of lying excuses to get rid of the others, till they can put their hand on him. Such a lad as you, my poor Beppo, is just the sort they want to make a soldier of; and you may depend on it, if they have half a chance, they will leave no stone unturned to get hold of you."

" I don't think that seems fair," said Beppo ; " a

fair lot is in the hands of the blessed Virgin and the saints; but when you come to picking and choosing, that is another matter."

The theory which thus limited the sphere of the influence of the spiritual powers was a curious one. But the Bella Luce theology was about contemporaneous with the Bella Luce system of vine-dressing, which, as we have seen, dated from before the Georgics.

The priest, however, only said in reply to Beppo's remonstrance :—

" Fair ! no : as if anything done by a robber government was likely to be fair ! It is all a mass of fraud, and violence, and tyranny, and iniquity, and godless impiety together."

It will be observed that the priest was very much more outspoken in his disaffection to the new government than he had been on the former occasion, when we had last the pleasure of meeting him. But Signor Sandro Bartoldi, the attorney, was present upon that occasion; a man from the town, not one who could be counted on as a stanch adherent of the good cause—in short, not a safe man at all. *Now*, the parish priest was speaking before none but members of his own mountain congregation, and he spoke out accordingly. He was not aware, however, how far the minds of the younger generation of his audience had slipped away from the old moorings, and drawn (who can say how ? Who can say how minds do draw nutriment from the surrounding atmosphere of thought, as silently as trees do from the air ?) somehow or other the material for the formation of new judgments and views of the world around them. The slowness of the peasant's mind, the submissive reverence which prevents him from ever "giving his priest an answer," as the vulgar phrase goes, and the unexpansive silence in which his intellect works, combine to prevent the parish clergy from being fully aware of the degree to which the minds of the rising generation of their flocks have emancipated themselves from their leading-strings. Not that there was the slightest danger that any one of the Bella Luce family would have made any use of the disaffected words uttered by their priest in a manner to be injurious to him. Besides that, this unhappy conscription question had, to a certain extent, thrown their minds into unison of sentiment with his once more. Otherwise Beppo had begun to form a shrewd opinion of his own, that the papal government was about as bad a one as it could be ; and that the new one, at all events, promised to be much better. But this conscription—it could not be denied that it was a bitter pill, and a staggering difficulty for the adherents of the new order of things.

"They do say," remarked old Paolo, in reply to the priest's last words, "that money may buy a man off if he is drawn. I should not wonder : there's few things that money can't do. But how can I find the means of buying Beppo off?—a poor working man like me. How can I do it, your reverence?—not to be able to keep a decent house over my head and pay my way, church dues and offerings and alms and masses as well. How can it be done ? It stands to reason it can't."

This was a desperate attempt on the part of the old farmer to know the worst, and ascertain whether he was expected to ransom his son at the cost of his hardly-saved and dearly-loved dollars. He knew very well that, if the priest said he must do so, he should have to do it. And he had thrown out a few topics for consideration to the *curato*—with the greatest tact and delicacy, as he flattered himself—which he thought might have the effect of influencing his decision upon the point in question.

The oracle spoke, and comforted him inexpressibly.

"There are few things, as you remark, Signor Vanni, which money judiciously employed may not do. Certainly it may bribe the wretches, who have usurped the territory and the power of the Holy Father, to disgorge the prey which they have seized in their infamous man-stealing. But I have very grave doubts of the lawfulness of thus expending money. I may say, indeed, that I am tolerably sure that it cannot be done without sin. And I have the means of knowing that such is the opinion of those in high places, and of the best authorities. To contribute money wilfully, not by compulsion, to the support of the excommunicated government is to give aid, countenance, and comfort to the enemies of our Holy Father, and persons under sentence of excommunication, which is very palpably damnable and mortal sin. But assuredly those who give their money for the purpose in question are guilty of doing this. My mind is quite clear upon the subject. I do not see how I should be able to give absolution, perhaps not even *in articulo mortis*, to a person lying under the guilt of this sin!"

"But," Beppo ventured to say timidly,—"but,

your reverence, if you go to fight for the new government yourself, is not it as bad as paying another to do it for you ? Must it not be equally sinful to go yourself ? And yet one or other of the two you must do."

" Must you ?" said the priest, drily.

" Well, your reverence, it seems that if you are drawn you must," said Beppo, simply.

" My notion is," said the priest, " that there will be a pretty considerable number of young men—God-fearing, well-educated young men— drawn for the conscription in this province who will do neither the one nor the other : who will neither suffer themselves to be torn away from their country to fight against their Holy Father and lawful sovereign, nor yet give money to his enemies to hire somebody else to do so." And as he spoke he rubbed his hands slowly together, and looked hard at Beppo.

The old father and mother looked from one to the other with watchful interest; the former much relieved in his mind, and feeling more than ever that Don Evandro was a second Daniel come to judgment.

" But it's no use for a man to say he won't go," rejoined Beppo. " Willy nilly, he must go.

If he won't go by his own will, he will be taken by force."

" Oh, no ! certainly ; it is of no use for a man to *say* he won't go—of no use at all.   It is not by *saying* that a man can do his duty to his God, and his Church, and his country.   Duty mostly needs something more than *saying*," returned the priest, with a very marked emphasis, and still looking hard at Beppo.

"I don't see it, your reverence," said Beppo, looking puzzled.   " What is a man to do, then ? "

" And yet it seems pretty clear, too," rejoined the curate.   " You say, if a man won't go, he will be taken by force ? "

" So I am told," said Beppo.

" Who will take him ? " asked the priest, Socratically.

" Why, the soldiers, I suppose ! " said Beppo, with very widely opened eyes.

" And where will they take him from ?   Where would they take *you* from, for instance, if you did not go to them ? " continued the priest, pushing on his catechism to its conclusion.

" If I were drawn, and did not go to give myself up at Fano, they would come here after me, and take me by force," said Beppo, begin-

ning to think that the priest was really unin-
formed upon the subject.

"Very true; they would come *here*—here to
Bella Luce! But suppose they did not find you
here?"

"Then they would take me wherever they
could find me. Why, bless your reverence's
heart, they aren't put off in that way."

"They would take you wherever they could
find you, no doubt. But suppose that they could
not find you at all?"

"What! If I were to put an end to myself,"
said poor Beppo, not appearing to be very much
startled by the suggestion; "but I thought, your
reverence, that that was not lawful to do in any
case?"

"Put an end to yourself? I am shocked at you,
Beppo! Unlawful?—of course it is. How could
you imagine I had such a thing in my thoughts?"

"Then I am sure I don't know, and it is not
for such as I am to guess, what *is* in your reverence's thoughts!" said Beppo, utterly puzzled.

"Why, my good friend, Beppo, you are not so
quick as I thought you. If you are drawn for
the conscription,—say, you don't go. The soldiers
come here to look for you;—don't find you.—

'We want Beppo Vanni,' say they; 'where is
he?'—'Really can't say,' says my friend, Signor
Paolo.—'Sure he is not in the house?' says the
officer.—'Quite sure,' says Signor Paolo. 'You
can search it if you like.' They do search it, but
they don't find Beppo Vanni. Then they come
away to Santa Lucia to see the *curato*, and try
what they can make out of him. 'We are come
to look for one Beppo Vanni, a parishioner of
yours, your reverence. Can you tell us where
we can find him?'—'He lives at Bella Luce,
when he is at home,' says his reverence; 'is he
not there now?'—'No, he is not there. But I
suppose your reverence knows where to find
him?' says the officer.—'If he is not there, he
must be out in the hills. There are many wolves
and wild boars, and such like, in our mountains,
but they are mostly very hard to catch,' says his
reverence; 'Beppo Vanni is very fond of hunting.
If you keep on the wolf's track, I dare say you
will find him; and I wish you a pleasant job of
it,' says his reverence.

"*Now* do you see it, friend Beppo?" asked the
priest, when he had concluded his little exposition, of which the latter part was delivered with
considerable dramatic effect.

"What, take to the hills *per bene?*" said Beppo, with a grim smile;—"for good and all," as an Englishman might have said.

"Ay, for *good*, assuredly!" said the priest. "But it would only·be for a short time, just till the secret was blown over, and the soldiers out of the country. That is what all the best men in the country will do. The excommunicated king will find that he will get very few men in Romagna, except the scum of the towns, to fight for him against the Holy Father."

"It looks like skulking, as if one had done something to be ashamed of, keeping out of the way in the hills in that fashion," said Beppo, thoughtfully.

"You will find, my friend, that all the shame will lie on the other side," returned the priest. "I tell you that all the best men in the country —those of them, at least, who have the misfortune to be drawn—will take to the hills."

"Your reverence spoke of the wolves and the wild boars," said Beppo, with a sigh; "every man's hand is against them, and they are hunted down."

"Yes," returned the priest, quickly; "they are hunted down because every man's hand *is* against them. But there is just the difference. Those

who take to the hills in this sacred cause will
have every good man for their friend. We priests,"
continued Don Evandro, with a grim smile of
conscious power, "are everywhere; and, do what
they will, they will never root us out. Wherever
there is a parish—what do I say?—wherever
there is Catholic soil, *there* is a Catholic priest.
And wherever there is a priest, those who are
homeless for the good cause will have a friend.
We shall have our eyes on those who are out in
the hills on account of this business. They will
not be let to want, neither for food nor for shelter;
no, nor for communication with their friends at
home," he added, looking hard at Beppo, with so
meaning a glance that it was all but a wink.

"And your reverence thinks that it would not
be for a very long time—that those who go out
into the hills will be able to return to their homes
after awhile?" asked Beppo, musingly.

"Of course. It stands to reason. Specially
those who live not in the towns, but in out-of-
the-way places like this. Why, we are almost
among the hills, as you may say, here. As soon
as this conscription business is over, the troops
will quit the country,—go to be shot down by
the Austrian cannon, or to cut the throats of

their brothers in Naples, or to be led to sacrilege against Rome, and be struck dead, perhaps, in the horrible act : what do I know ? They will be marched away; and then the country will be quiet, till God sees fit in His mercy to restore the lawful and rightful government ; and when *that* day comes, as come it surely will before long, those who have refused at any cost to bear arms against their Holy Father will have cause to bless themselves, and thank their good fortune."

" And your reverence thinks there would be means of holding communication with—with one's friends at home, or—or in the towns ? "

" No doubt about that," said the priest, again looking, with peculiar intelligence, hard at Beppo. " We shall take care about that. There would be no lack of means of communication. Any man in the hills for this cause might know, day by day, if he cared about it—which is hardly likely —what was the news in the towns."

" That would be a great thing, certainly," said Beppo, meditating, and seeming to speak more to himself than to the priest.

" What ! I suppose your visit to Signor Sandro's house yesterday has made you wish to hear from him again, eh ? "

" Yes !—no ! That is, your reverence, not
from him particularly," replied Beppo, far too
simple to tell a lie, even when it was put into
his mouth for him by the person to whom it was
to be told.

" Ah ! I see !" said the priest, pretending to
misunderstand him ; " not from *him*, perhaps.
I am told that Lisa Bartoldi is becoming one
of the most charming girls in Fano—immensely
improved of late, and greatly sought after. No
wonder, with her expectations. It is a pity her
father should have let some of those scamps of
officers come round her. But that will be all over
as soon as they are out of the country—pests as
they are ! But Lisa is a prudent girl, and is very
safe not to commit herself." (The priest did not
guess that Lisa had been perfectly confidential
with Beppo on the subject of her loves with the
captain of Bersaglieri.) " Would to Heaven," he
continued, " that as much could be said for that
unfortunate Giulia ! I have almost reproached
myself for having advised that the proposal of
Signor Sandro to send her to Fano should be
accepted for her. But God knows I acted for the
best, and to the best of my judgment. Who could
have thought that a girl so brought up would

have gone to the bad so shamefully, and that in so short a time?" And the priest lifted his hands and eyes to heaven, or, at least, to the ceiling of the farmhouse kitchen, as he spoke. "But the fact is," he added, dropping his eyes with a meek, resigned sigh, "that when a girl is thoroughly bad nothing can save her. A heartless, false girl is, and must be, lost, whether in town or country."

The supper, of which Don Evandro had partaken with the family, had been finished long ago. It had consisted merely of the *minestra,* a bit of cheese afterwards, and a flask of the farmer's Bella Luce wine. But Signora Sunta had been assailed by no false shame, and had made no efforts to increase her bill of fare, and no boasting excuses to the priest any more than to one of the family. For he was not a guest from the city, but a fellow-villager, who was one of themselves. The supper therefore had not taken long. And as soon as it was over, *la* Sunta had without apology taken up the one *lumino,* or tall brass Roman lamp, which had stood on the supper-table, and had gone with it about her household affairs, leaving her husband and sons and their guest to smoke their cigars and have

their talk by the light of the May moon which
streamed in through the open kitchen-door. Old
Paolo had fallen asleep soon after the conversation had reached the point at which it had been
authoritatively decided that it would be wicked of
him to pay out money. Since that, the talk had
been entirely between Beppo and the priest, and
Carlo had been an attentive listener. It was fortunate for Beppo that they were sitting so nearly
in the dark, for he felt that it would have been
impossible otherwise for him to have concealed
from the ever-watchful eye of the priest the
agitation and misery which the last words of the
latter were causing him. They did but confirm
his own impressions of the day before. But then
those impressions had been the result of indignation—of the things which he had seen with his
eyes! His eyes no longer saw them! His indignation had begun to wane! The impressions had
become less forcible and distinct. It was growing
more possible for him to persuade himself that he
exaggerated matters—that he himself had been to
blame—that there might still be a possibility of
hope for him, in short. But now the words of
Don Evandro rudely threw down again all the
fabric he was once more striving to raise, and cut

off like a blighting March wind the new green shoots that his love, which would not be killed, was again putting forth. The pain was very agonising to him, and it was a relief to him that it was too dark for the priest to see his features.

In truth, the darkness concealed little or nothing from the priest's knowledge, if it did from his eyes. He knew perfectly well the effect of what he was saying, as well as the surgeon knows the sensations of the patient under his knife.

But the operation was not over—Beppo had more to suffer yet.

"What mischief, then, has Giulia been getting into in the city, your reverence?" asked Carlo. "I am not surprised, for one, for I always thought her a bad one. I never knew her to stay for the litanies after vespers, not once last year; and I must know, for I never missed them all the winter!"

Don Evandro knew and understood all the low hypocrisy of this speech quite as perfectly as any man could; nevertheless he approved of it; thought it the desirable kind of tone for a young man, and considered that it showed Carlo to be the sort of man that was needed for a good subject and a good churchman. So a woman who

receives a compliment which she knows to be
insincere may yet be pleased with it, as indicating
the desire on the part of the payer of it to please
her.

" Ah ! it is a bad business—a very bad business
—I am afraid ! Part of my object in going into
the city on Saturday was to make inquiries and
ascertain if there might be any hope of saving
her. I fear me !—I fear that there is nothing to
be done !"

The priest, not calculating on the chivalrous
generosity of heart of the man he was speaking to,
or rather at—(as how should he calculate on
what he could not conceive ?)—was overshooting
his mark a little in the excess of his calumnious
statements. For the idea of Giulia in danger and
in trouble at once began to make love assume the
mask of pity, and an evident desire to save and
protect her began to override and overpower, for
the moment, his own infinite misery.

" What has she been up to ?" asked Carlo again.

" Oh, up to !" said the priest, hesitating as if
unwilling to speak out. " What mischief do unprincipled girls get into when they get the opportunity ? It is the old story. There is the town,
too, full of soldiers, reprobate profligates, without

religion or principle of any kind ! It is destruction to the character of any decent girl to be known to have any communication with them, or be seen in their company, and this abandoned girl has formed an intimacy with one of the most notorious blackguards in the whole lot of them !"

Beppo groaned audibly, as he acknowledged to himself that his first impressions with regard to Corporal Tenda had been but too just.

" What ! you don't mean," said Carlo, eagerly, " that she has—taken up with any one in particular you know—so as to lose her character, you know ? "

" Character ! It will be well for her if that is all she has lost ! Character ! She will never be able to hold her head up in this country any more ! The best thing that could happen to her would be to follow the blackguard for good and all, and let the disgrace she has brought upon her name be forgotten. But he is no doubt too knowing a rascal for that."

" But he may be made to answer for his conduct — to do what is right by her !" said Beppo, breathing hard and clenching his fists.

The priest could not see the action; but he knew from Beppo's voice all that was passing in

his mind. And he considered for a moment or
two, during which he took a rapid survey of all
the circumstances of the case with masterly com-
prehensiveness, whether it might be good policy
to bring these men face to face with a result that
might probably in one way or other make Carlo
the heir to the Bella Luce homestead and savings.
But he gave up the idea as involving too many
possibilities of miscarriage. So he replied :—

"How make him answer for his conduct? His
officers are as bad as he. There is no law to touch
him. And to resort to unchristian violence would
bring destruction upon your own soul, in all probability without injuring him."

"Who is the man?" asked Carlo.

"One Tenda, a corporal; a low Piedmontese
blackguard—one of the worst characters in the
army, I am told."

"A Piedmontese too!" exclaimed Carlo, with
unaffected disgust; "to think of Giulia taking up
with a Piedmontese, of all the men in the world!
Why, it is against nature!"

"I must say that I think Signor Sandro has
been very much to blame," continued the priest,
"in not making himself better acquainted with
the character of the woman with whom he placed

Giulia—a retired actress, I learn! It is true that, as far as I can hear, there is nothing to be said against the woman now. She has become reconciled to the Church, and there is no more to be said about it. But Signor Sandro might have known that such a woman was not likely to be a safe protectress for such a girl as Giulia."

" But, then, who would have guessed that our Giulia would need so much protecting?" said Carlo.

"That is true, too, *figliuolo mio*," said the priest. " Well, I must be thinking of walking homewards. It is getting late. Good night, Signor Paolo. I need not wish it you, for you have been taking a slice of it already—a calm conscience makes an easy pillow. Good night, Signor Beppo. We shall have some further conversation as soon as the result of this detestable drawing is known. Good-night."

So the priest set out on his moonlight walk to Santa Lucia, satisfactorily reflecting that he had —he could hardly doubt—deprived Victor Emmanuel of one of the likeliest soldiers in Romagna; and had, in all probability, put an end to all inconveniences arising from love-passages between Beppo and Giulia.

CHAPTER VII.

THE BAD NUMBER.

HE communal lists were all made out. There was very little interest attached to that part of the business. It was a matter of course that all except the few names of those who were utterly out of the question should appear in them. Nor did they, when completed, afford to the inhabitants of each commune any even approximative indication of the amount of chances for and against them. For this depended upon the proportion of the number of men required to the number of those liable,— not in each commune, but in the entire military district; and though a tolerably fair estimate of this might be known to the authorities in the provincial capital, the *contadino* inhabitants of each rustic commune were wholly ignorant upon the subject.

So the lists were made out and sent to the town, and the population hardly yet realised the nature and nearness of the misfortune which was about to fall on them.

Then came news that the day for the drawing was fixed. It was a day very near at hand—a day towards the end of May.

Early on the fateful morning the men began to arrive from all sides in the city. They came up in droves from the different communes, and the comparison of them to cattle driven to the slaughter-house was too obvious to escape many of the men themselves, and was with malicious bitterness suggested to them by many a parish priest, as his parishioners were starting from their obscure little villages in the hills, on their un-welcome errand. The appearance of the poor fellows when they arrived in the city was also suggestive enough of the comparison. They came with heavy steps and reluctant limbs, not knowing what was going to happen, or what they were to do first, stupidly jostling each other in the crowded streets, and vacantly staring with great wide eyes at the preparations that had been made for the drawing.

Some few parties were accompanied by their

priests; but for the most part those gentlemen did not choose to take any overt share in the matter, or to sanction it by their presence. They preferred to do their part respecting it in the background. A greater number of the rustic parties were accompanied by the older men, and some had women with them.

If the population had looked forward to the day with terror and vague misgiving, the authorities had not been altogether free from apprehension with regard to it. It was well known how very repugnant the measure was to the almost entire population. The Government were well aware that this feeling was stimulated and worked on to the utmost of their power by the clergy, and it was feared that disturbances might take place. A considerable force of military, therefore, were under arms at different points of the little city; and as the rustics, decked out for the sacrifice in their best holiday trim, arrived in the town, they saw bodies of soldiers drawn up, as if to show them specimens of what they were about to become.

In the large open piazza of the city—and at Fano the principal piazza is a remarkably large and fine one—the crowd was chiefly assembled in front of the *palazzo pubblico*—the town-hall, as we should say. For there the drawing, which was to award despair or the rejoicing of escape to many a homestead, was to take place, in the largest hall of the building. The operation was to be conducted in the presence of the civic authorities. The military powers took no part in the matter at its present stage, seeing that they were interested only in the due forthcoming of the prescribed number of men. Who those men were to be was of interest to the population and to their communal and municipal authorities, but of no interest to the military authorities. They demanded their pound of flesh ; but left the cutting of it to the discretion and convenience of the patient.

It was a curious and interesting thing to thread that anxious crowd, and mark the varying expression of the different groups ! There were reckless faces of men, on whom, if the lot should fall, the service would gain little, and the country lose as little. There were stolid-looking boors, who seemed scarcely more capable of appreciating the nature of the change which threatened them than the great meek-eyed, dove-coloured oxen which were their most habitual companions. There

were spruce-looking well-to-do youths, the hope
and stay of well-regulated households, anxiously
talking over the chances of the fateful urn with
downcast elders. There were yet more interesting
groups, in which an aged mother, a sister, or one
holding a yet tenderer relationship to the youth
menaced with what to her was almost equivalent
to death, were the principal figures.

Beppo was there alone. The other young men
from his commune had come up together; but he
had felt too miserable and down-hearted to come
with them. Yet there was little in their comrade-
ship, that would have jarred upon his melancholy
mood. The lads of the French rural district,
though abhorring the conscription to the full as
much as these Romagnoles could do, will go to the
fatal urn singing and laughing, hiding the death in
their hearts from every eye, and from their own
consciousness as far as noise and bluster, and
" Dutch courage," will enable them to do so. But
the simpler, more genuine, less vain, and less self-
conscious Italian nature makes no such attempt.
They go to the drawing miserable and dejected,
and they make no attempt to conceal the fact.
One of the most touchingly melancholy of all the
popular melodies I ever heard, is the song of the

Tuscan conscripts torn from their country by the first Napoleon, which is still remembered in the country districts of Tuscany. Nothing can be further from any pretence of enthusiasm or desire for French " glory."

But Beppo had a far worse heartache than any of them,—a heartache which he could not discuss with any of them; and he had therefore come up from Bella Luce alone. He was standing at the further side of the piazza, opposite to the *palazzo pubblico*, leaning against the corner of a house, which makes the angle of a street there opening into the piazza, with his broad-leafed *contadino* hat drawn over his brows, moodily and almost absently watching the moving crowd in front of him, and the floating of the tri-coloured banner which adorned the front of the palazzo.

The drawing was appointed to commence at eleven. But nothing ever yet, in Italy, commenced at the hour named for the commencement of it. It was now past eleven, and the crowd were patiently waiting, in no wise displeased or surprised at being detained there. The *gonfaloniere* was still taking his cup of coffee at some café; or the official who kept the key of the hall, in which the drawing was to take place, had

mislaid, and could not find it; or the clerk who
should have prepared the balloting urn, and
who had had a month or more to do some ten
minutes' job, had not yet completed it; or everything was perfectly ready, everybody assembled,
and there was no reason whatsoever for not proceeding to business directly,—except that it is
always pleasanter to put off doing anything than
to do it, and it was still possible to put off the
beginning of the present business in hand a little
longer. Any one of these, or fifty other such
reasons, would have been quite sufficient. It was
half-past eleven; there were no signs of any
beginning being made yet, and nobody of any
sort, neither of those who had to operate, nor of
those who had to be operated on, was, in the least
degree, either angry, or surprised, or impatient.
The groups of peasants stood about the wide
piazza as patiently as if they were ruminating
like their own oxen; and now and then some
official came to the balcony in front of the great
central window of the *palazzo pubblico*, gazed
out for awhile on the crowd below, and retired
again.

At last, at about half-an-hour after noon, a bell
was rung as a signal that the business of the day

really was about to commence. There was a swaying movement amongst the crowd, and some pressed on to enter the building and ascend the great stairs into the principal hall of it, in which the drawing was to take place; and others hung back, as lacking courage to look their destiny in the face.

It is not absolutely necessary that any one of those liable to the conscription should come to the drawing. He comes there for his own satisfaction and not for that of the government. He may, if he please, commission any relative or friend to draw for him, or failing this, if the individual does not present himself, nor anybody on his behalf, the *gonfaloniere* puts his own hand into the urn and draws a number for him.

The operation is performed in public. Any one may enter the hall who pleases; and there generally is a large concourse of the friends of those about to draw, or of merely curious loungers. On the occasion in question a great number of the townspeople, who had no especial interest in the proceedings, had gathered in the hall. For the Fano *beau-monde* have not many sources of amusement, and the conscription at all events offered them the means of getting rid of a day—

an advantage not to be despised in one of those little Adriatic cities.

At the upper end of the huge hall, within a space railed off, is a long green baize-covered table, on the middle of which is the urn, containing a quantity of folded slips of paper, all scrupulously alike, equal in number to the number of men liable to serve. Each of these contains simply a number, from one up to the last of the series. The *gonfaloniere*, who is equivalent to our mayor, sits on a somewhat raised chair immediately behind this apparatus. By his side are municipal councillors, and close behind him is the *pubblicatore*, the publisher or crier, whose duty it is to announce the names with their numbers, as they are drawn. The patient puts his hand into the urn, draws it forth, holding one slip of paper between his fingers; he unfolds it himself, reads himself first his fate, then hands it to the *gonfaloniere*, who reads and passes it to the *pubblicatore* to be cried aloud; after which it is duly registered, and then sent to the printer.

The hall of the Fano *palazzo pubblico* was crowded, as has been said, in great part by townspeople who had no interest in the ceremony save one of simple curiosity. Towards the upper part of the large space—which had probably been used as a banqueting-hall in the old days, when there was more of feasting and less of fasting done in Italy than in these latter centuries—there was at a height of some feet from the floor of the hall a sort of tribune, or small gallery, enclosed by a light parapet of iron scroll-work, the elegance of which plainly declared it to be the work of the sixteenth century. In all probability the place thus contrived had been intended for the accommodation of musicians during the Fano feastings. Now it afforded a very convenient place for any one who wished to look on at the proceedings in the body of the hall, without being exposed to contact with the crowd which thronged the floor.

Of course the small privilege of occupying this sort of private box at the representation of the tragi-comedy about to come off, was in the gift of the members of the municipality, of whom our friend Signor Alessandro Bartoldi, the attorney, was one of the most active and influential. It was of course also, under these circumstances, that the desirable place in question should be at the disposition of the fair Lisa. And there accordingly was Lisa, accompanied by her friend Giulia, between whom and the attorney's daughter a considerable intimacy had sprung up out of the frequent visits of the latter to the house of *la* Dossi, to which she was drawn by—the reader knows what attraction.

La Dossi herself had declined to accompany the girls. She was very far from locomotive in her habits, and had much preferred, when allowing Giulia to accompany her friend to the drawing, to undertake herself, in a spirit of thoughtful and experimental investigation, the preparation of the day's dinner. So there, amid some other lady connections of the municipal magnates, was the superb Giulia, by far the most noticeable person in the little pulpit, or gallery, or whatever it may be called, with the pale and delicate little Lisa by her side, each admirably serving the office of a foil to the beauty of the other : for though poor little Lisa was terribly eclipsed by the magnificently-developed and brilliantly-coloured beauty of the daughter of the Apennine, the pale little town-bred girl was not without her beauty too, of a kind more attractive to some men, perhaps, than the sun-steeped gorgeousness of the other.

What Giulia's feelings may have been, when after her unpleasant interview with Beppo he refused to enter *la* Signora Dossi's dwelling, and

she told him to please himself in the matter;
whether the somewhat boisterous gaiety with
which she and Corporal Tenda laughed and talked,
while Lisa and Captain Brilli were more quietly
engaged in their flirtation in the sitting-room, was
as completely and genuinely enjoyed by her as by
the corporal ; whether, when she found herself
alone in her room that night, there may have been
a little of what in medical phrase is termed "re-
action;" and, finally, whether this day of the
drawing may have been looked forward to by her
with something more of interest than attaches to
a mere spectacle of the interests of others, need
not at present be too curiously inquired into.
This much, at least, is certain, that if anybody
had thought to spy any, the smallest sign or
symptom of willow-wearing, or down-heartedness
of any sort, in Giulia's face or bearing, as she sate
by the side of her little friend on the occasion of
the drawing, they would have been, agreeably or
disagreeably as the case may have been, but very
certainly, disappointed.   She sat there radiant in
beauty, chattering with Lisa and others around
her—the *contadina* shyness and taciturnity having
been already got rid of under the discipline and
forcing process of her town life.

The process of drawing began. The city of
Fano stands in the midst of a rich and populous
region; and the number to be drawn was large.
The number of men to be furnished to the army
of Italy from that district was not far short of a
hundred. But to ensure the certainty of obtaining that number of efficient and unobjectionable
soldiers, at least three times that number would
be required by the military authorities to present
themselves on the day fixed for the medical examination. The probability would be that the
last sixty or seventy of these,—that is to say, those
holding the highest numbers—would be tolerably
safe. Those ranging from a hundred to a hundred
and fifty or so, would be pretty sure to be called
on to supply the place of those rejected (or those
who might have made themselves scarce) among
the first hundred. The fate of those holding the
numbers between, say, a hundred and fifty and
two hundred and twenty or thirty, would be very
doubtful, the chances of escape becoming greater,
of course, as the higher numbers were reached.
Though all those liable draw their numbers from
the same urn, and when drawn form part of
one and the same numerically-arranged roll, the
operation is performed commune by commune.

The young men from each commune come up in a body and draw in alphabetical order.

Santa Lucia was not among the communes that came first to the urn.

The business went on regularly, and the spectators had plenty of occupation and amusement watching the look and bearing of the men as they drew, and as they read their fate. The most remarkable feature of the scene was the absence of bravado. The young fellows who came up to the urn for the decision whether they were to be enrolled among the heroes and defenders of their country, or were to return to the plough, made no attempt whatever to conceal their strong preference for the latter destiny. The presence of female relatives and friends, and the "galaxy of beauty in the gallery" produced no effect of this kind whatever. The old jousting herald's reminder to the brave knights, that "bright eyes behold your deeds," would have been quite thrown away on the occasion.

The naïve acceptance, admission, and avowal of feelings and affections of all kinds is a very noticeable and curious trait in the Italian character. Sometimes this striking peculiarity seems to our more reserved and secretive northern nature

to approach to cynicism; and sometimes to be
evidence of an open unaffected simplicity of character worthy of the golden age. The fact is,
that in all respects the Italian nature does par-
take far more than any other of the characteristics
of the golden age of childhood.

The majority accordingly of those who drew the
lower numbers made no effort to conceal their
chagrin—in one or two instances rising to really
tragic manifestations of despair. More than one
stout hulking fellow retired from the table sobbing; nor was he felt by any one present to disgrace himself or forfeit their sympathy by such
a display of his emotions. On the contrary, those
who displayed the most striking and visible signs
of grief were deemed to grieve most deeply, and
were accordingly most pitied. In a few cases,
when it was well known that the drawer would
serve by proxy, and that his interest in the matter
was only one of money, his disgust at drawing a
number which put him to the expense of pro-
viding a substitute was a matter rather of merri-
ment than of sympathy to the bystanders. In
several cases doltish stupidity seemed to prevent
all manifestation of feeling and even of interest
in the matter. They came up to the urn, did as

they were bid absolutely with the slow, lumbering, impassible docility of their cattle, without seeming to comprehend the nature of the consequences which had been decided for them.

To those meanwhile who had already drawn numbers ranging from about a hundred and fifty or so to some two hundred and twenty or thirty, the remainder of the drawing was still a matter of anxious interest. For of course their own chances very materially depended on the sort of men who drew the numbers below them. And every time a low number was drawn by some man who it was pretty clear would be rejected by the medical examiners, a murmur of disappointment might be heard among the crowd. And now and then the proclamation of some name with a number that manifestly condemned the drawer of it to serve, was received with significant interchange of glances among such of the doubtful ones as knew him, which might very easily be interpreted to express their shrewd doubts whether the individual in question would be of any avail to stand between them and the danger.

" *He* is no good ! " one of these anxious watchers would whisper to another, while a glance and an expressive gesture, performed by some scarcely visible movement of finger, eyebrow or shoulder, said clearly enough to the friend addressed that Victor Emmanuel would have to look *very* sharp if he meant his army to be increased by *that* drawing.

And many were even then at work with all their mental faculties deciding the momentous question whether they should "take to the hills" or not. For if such a step were to be adopted, it must be done in the interval between the drawing and the medical examination. After the final making up of the roll in accordance with the decisions then arrived at on each separate case, the men whose names are on it are no more lost sight of by the military authorities. Between the first drawing and the examination they return to their villages, though they are bound not to quit them. And it is in the course of those days, generally from about fourteen to twenty in number, that the desertions take place. Those who had drawn low numbers, had before this made up their minds what they would do in case of their drawing such. But with those who were in the category of the doubtful, it was a matter of anxious question, and mature consideration of the chances as affected by the nature and cha-

racter of the men below them, whether they
should stay and abide the chances of the examination or not.

Never was medical insight into the constitution
and temperament of one's neighbours so valuable.

At last it came to the turn of the Santa Lucia
lads to march up to the table.

They came up the hall, some eight or ten in
number, fine looking fellows all of them. The
hill populations give but a small percentage of
the medical rejections. They are the sort of
men the military authorities want; and to get
at whom they would willingly reject the townsmen wholesale, if they could find any excuse for
doing so. All that little company from the
Apennine village of Santa Lucia were fine men,
but Beppo Vanni was conspicuous among them
both by his superior stature and by the comeli-
ness of his features.

"There's a fellow for a sergeant-major!" said
Captain Brilli to Corporal Tenda, who was in the
hall with him, amid the crowd of lookers on, as
the little Santa Lucia squad marched up the
floor. "I hope we shall nab him!"

"Why, that's my old acquaintance, Signor
Beppo Vanni. I little thought, when I told him

that we should meet again, how soon there would
be a chance of our making so much closer an
acquaintance with him. But I am afraid there
is not much prospect of making a soldier of him,
captain. His father is a rich man, I am told."

"Why, how do you know anything about it?
And how upon earth came he to be an acquaintance of yours?"

"Don't you remember, Signor Capitano, my
telling you of the visit we had that Sunday, at
the house of *la* Signora Dossi? That is the
angry gentleman who was as jealous as a Turk
because he found me in company with the superb
Giulia. He is a cousin of hers, it seems; and
from what I saw then, he would very much like
to be nearer related to her; but I saw no signs
of any similar intention on the part of *la bella*
Giulia. She did not appear inclined to have anything to say to him."

"Oh yes, I remember all about it now," said
the captain, scanning Beppo with his eye as he
spoke. And yet," he added, "he is not the sort
of fellow a pretty girl would turn away from. I
should not much fancy having Signor Beppo
Vanni for a rival myself, corporal!"

"Oh, as for that," said the little corporal, drawing himself up, "it's not always the big hulking fellows that the girls like best—not at all! And besides, Master Beppo did not go the right way to make any girl fancy him. He was as savage as a bear, and seemed more inclined to blow her up, the poor little darling! by way of making love, than anything else. Now Giulia is not the girl to stand that sort of thing. She is as good as gold. But she won't stand preaching from her cousin Beppo, if I know her."

"And she will stand a different sort of talk from a smart corporal of Bersaglieri, eh?"

"Not in the way of anything free and easy, you understand, captain. Lord bless you! She is a real good girl, I tell you. I should as soon think of saying anything that one does not say to an honest woman, to *la* Giulia, as I should to the colonel's wife. She will laugh as much as you please; but all right and proper, mind you!"

"Well, yes; I suppose so. *La* Lisa says that she is a good girl. But I don't feel so sure about her caring nothing for that strapping cousin of hers."

"That for her cousin!" said the little corporal, snapping his fingers. "We shall see, Signor Capitano, some of these fine days."

"One of these fine days, I suppose, when the

old uncle at Cuneo has hopped the twig, and the corporal has turned his sword into a ploughshare, eh ? " said the captain, laughing.

" Well, don't you think I might do worse, Signor Capitano ? Did you ever see a better mistress for the little farm at Cuneo ? "

" Have you proposed that enviable position to Giulia, *la magnifica*, yet, corporal ? "

" No, not yet ; but I have serious thoughts of doing so—freehold land, every foot of it ! Why should I not ? There's plenty would jump at it."

" No doubt. But you would have to jump at *la* Giulia. I swear she is a head taller than you are, corporal ! "

" Not a bit of it ! Parcel of nonsense ! We are exactly of a height, she and I," said the little man, holding up his head.

" Have you measured ? "

" No ; but I can see, I suppose."

" A corporal of Bersaglieri ought to know that one always sights a mark less above one's eye than it is. I'd wager she is taller than you."

" Stuff and nonsense ! Look, he is going to draw now ! "

Beppo, in passing up the hall, had caught sight of Giulia in her tribune, and no doubt she had

marked him as he walked up, a head taller than
his companions. But no mark of recognition had
taken place between them, and the only effect that
the knowledge of her presence had produced upon
him was to make him feel as if he were walking
in a dream, and as if all the scene around him
were hazy and unintelligible. His eyes swam, and
there was a buzzing in his ears, and he seemed to
himself to have a difficulty in bringing his mind
to bear upon the business in hand sufficiently to
go through with his share in it. As for any care
about the result, or any care about anything save
the fact that Giulia sat there looking on at the
ceremony he was called to take part in, and that
though a few yards of space only separated them,
there was an impassable gulf between them which
must part them for ever — he was wholly dead
to it !

He felt as if he were staggering as he stepped
up to the table, and the last among the Santa
Lucia men (for they drew alphabetically) put his
hand into the urn. The evident trouble he was in
was of course attributed by the spectators to his
dread of the chance which the urn was about to
award him. Others had in different ways showed
as much emotion, and had excited the pity of the

crowd. And now there was a little hush of anxiety and sympathy, especially among the female part of the assembly, with the magnificently handsome *contadino*.

He put his hand into the urn, and drawing forth a cartel, handed it in a dreamy sort of manner, without opening it, as he should have done, to the presiding magistrate.

"Read your number," said the *gonfaloniere*.

Beppo opened and read, "ONE HUNDRED AND ONE!"

The announcement did not seem to produce any visible effect upon him. He continued in the same sort of stunned dreamy condition as before. He passed the paper to the *gonfaloniere*, who, after casting his eye on it, handed it to the *pubblicatore*, who held it up before the people, crying out at the same time,

"GIUSEPPE VANNI; ONE HUNDRED AND ONE!"

Of course this was a certain condemnation to the ranks.

There was a perceptible and momentary stir among the audience which seemed in some degree to recall Beppo to himself. He cast his eyes, despite himself, towards the place where Giulia had been sitting, and perceived that her conspicuously noble head and bust were no longer in the spot which they had filled, and that there was a little movement among the women who crowded the tribune.

His look however was but momentary, and he turned from the table, together with the others from his commune, one only of whom besides himself had drawn a bad number, and slowly made his way to the bottom of the hall, and out of the *palazzo pubblico.*

"*Per Bacco!* we have caught our sergeant-major," said Corporal Tenda to Captain Brilli, "and to judge by the look of him, I should say that he knows his father don't mean to fork out to save him!"

"He didn't seem to like it, poor devil!" returned the captain; "but I say, corporal, while you, like a zealous officer, were looking after the recruits, I was looking somewhere else, and I'll tell you what I saw. I saw the future mistress of the little freehold farm at Cuneo turn as pale as death when her cousin drew his bad number, and then she and *la* Lisa left the tribune all in a hurry. I tell you again, I should not like Sergeant-Major Beppo Vanni for a rival with his superb cousin, if I was Corporal Tenda."

"Ah! bah! I have seen them together. She can't endure him, I tell you. Turned pale! I dare say—the room is infernally hot!"

Beppo purposed, as far as he could be said in the condition in which he was to purpose anything, to find his way to the inn, get his horse, and start at once on his return to Bella Luce. He had not been near Signor Sandro's house, and had with much difficulty forced himself to abstain from the temptation of passing down the street in which *la* Dossi's house was situated. It would be only pain to him to look on that fine big house again ; yet he was sorely tempted to do so.

As he was passing out from the door of the *palazzo pubblico* he encountered the little attorney himself, full of business and in a great bustle.

"Oh, Signor Beppo, so you are hit! Never mind it, man. Signor Paolo can afford it, and never know the difference. It is a very different matter with some of these poor fellows. What! cheer up, man ! Why have you not been in.to see us? Lisa is up in the hall there. Ah, I know one that had a lump in her throat when you drew the bad number. You'll come home with us ?"

" If you will excuse me, Signor Sandro, I think I

must go home. They will be anxious to hear the upshot of the drawing, you know."

" Well, as you will. But cheer up, man! I shall see you soon, no doubt ; for you will be coming in about the finding of a substitute. By-the-bye, have you seen your cousin, Giulia? From all I hear, I did better for her than I thought, in bringing her into the city. I am told she and a certain Signor Tenda, a corporal in the Bersaglieri, are likely to make a match of it! A very decent man, I hear, though he is but a corporal, and likely one day to have a pretty little property of his own."

" I have seen nothing of her," replied Beppo, in a tone of profound dejection. " Good evening, Signor Sandro."

" Well, if you won't stay, I must say good evening, I suppose. A pleasant ride home !"

Beppo went plodding heavily through the streets, with his eyes fixed to the pavement, till just at the corner of the lane in which his inn was situated, he was roused by hearing himself suddenly called by his name, and looking up found himself face to face with Lisa and Giulia.

It was Lisa who had called to him. She had done so in spite of Giulia's earnest remonstrances and entreaties to her, by look and gesture, not to speak.

"Oh, Signor Vanni! I declare I believe you were going to pass us without speaking to us. Ah! you little think what a pain it was to us when we saw the horrid number. Not but what Signor Paolo will get a substitute, of course!"

"It is not his intention to do so. Addio! Signora Lisa! I am in haste to return home."

And he was turning to leave them, without further speech.

"But, Signor Beppo," said Lisa, in a tone of petulant remonstrance, "are you going away without saying a word to your cousin!"

"I said too many the last time I had the—the pain of seeing her!"

Giulia had continued all this time with her eyes fixed to the ground, and gave no sign of having heard anything that had been said. But at these last words she looked up suddenly for half an instant, and seemed as if she was going to speak. But she changed her purpose, and said nothing, again casting down her eyes to the pavement.

"Ah! Signor Beppo!" rejoined Lisa, "I wish you could have seen her when you drew that odious number! I could hardly get her from the hall."

"Lisa, what nonsense are you talking!" said Giulia, indignantly. "Are you mad? You know yourself that I was fainting from the heat."

"I am not the least likely to suppose that it was from any other cause!" said Beppo, with icy sternness.

"But, Signor Beppo," said poor Lisa, beseechingly, and beginning to fear that she had done more harm than good by stopping him in his walk, "you don't really mean that Signor Paolo will suffer you to join the army?"

"I neither know nor care, Signora Lisa, what may become of me. My life is a weary burthen to me. I would as soon be rid of it by an Austrian bullet as in any other way. I am a lost and ruined man. My heart has been broken by a cruel, a faithless, false, and worthless woman!"

Lisa, whose arm was within Giulia's, felt her tremble all over, as these words passed Beppo's lips. She again raised her face, which was as pale as death, as if to speak; but again she checked herself, and remained silent.

"I despise myself," continued Beppo, raising his hand as if in denunciation, and inspired by strong passion with an eloquence that no one who knew him would have believed him capable of; "I despise myself for still caring for one so monstrously false and so vile! I despise myself; yet I know that I can cease to do so only by ceasing to live; and I pray to God that he will soon give me that release!"

He turned from them and rushed down the little lane, at the corner of which Lisa had stopped him.

Giulia stood for a minute, rigid yet tottering, like some tall column mined at its base and swaying to its fall, and then, without word or sound, fell heavily on the pavement.

END OF VOL. I.

BRADBURY AND EVANS, PRINTERS, WHITEFRIARS.

www.ingramcontent.com/pod-product-compliance
Lightning Source LLC
Chambersburg PA
CBHW060552030726
47498CB00005B/1363